WEB OF DESTINIES

A novel

PASCAL INARD

Cover design by Amélie Inard

Published by Happy Paw Prints, PO Box 2604, Cheltenham 3192, Australia

ISBN: 978-0-9874259-1-1

Chapter One

8th May 2012, Paris.

"Madame Alençon, I'm going to have to use a ventouse to help the baby come out," Guillaume said to the mother-to-be who had been pushing for an hour with no result. She had been admitted to the hospital during the night with excruciating contractions and had been administered an epidural.

There was no other place Docteur Guillaume Chambon wanted to be on this public holiday than l'hôpital de Pitié-Salpétrière, one of the largest hospitals in Paris. Today was going to be a busy day. Spring was a peak time for births and some mothers asked to be induced so their child could be born on Victory day, some calling their baby Victoire or Victor.

Just as he got the vacuum device that was going to assist the delivery, the baby's head appeared. Guillaume put it back and came back to his exhausted patient, while the midwife exhorted her to continue pushing. A speedy delivery ensued, and Guillaume put the baby boy on his mother's chest, to the sound of laughter and exclamations from his relieved grandmother and father.

What a wonderful way to come into the world.

Madame Alençon looked at her newborn son with tenderness while he was feeding, before the nurse interrupted their first moment of togetherness to carry out the usual tests and dress him. "Thank you Docteur, you've done a wonderful job. It means a lot to us after what we've been through. My husband had lost hope after my miscarriage and I kept telling him that we should try again. He was anxious for me, so he made me promise it would be our last attempt. And now here he is, isn't he beautiful?"

Guillaume nodded. The smile on her face wasn't the only reason he had chosen to work on this public holiday. Helping mothers to give birth numbed the pain that this day brought up. He had a wound in his soul that was acutely painful on the anniversary of his sister Bénédicte's death. It happened twenty-two years ago, but it seemed like yesterday.

Bénédicte had gone to Laos with her Laotian husband Pathana, and had died in labour. Guillaume saw himself ready to blow out the ten candles on his cake, picking up the phone expecting his sister to sing *Happy Birthday,* and instead hearing the bad news from her brother-in-law Keona. He had dropped the phone, unable to repeat to his parents what he had heard.

Claire, the head midwife who had been on the night shift, had waited for Guillaume to come back from the delivery room to give him a briefing before going home. "Madame Dussieux is upset, her contractions started during the night and Docteur Gallais has gone to Bretagne for the long week-end. He's the only one she trusts."

"Is she full term?"

"Only one week early."

"How dilated is she?"

"Five centimetres. She's in delivery room two, but the other doctors are busy."

Guillaume shrugged. "Well, she'll have to do with me. What else?"

"Remember Madame Ravel?"

"Yes, the all-organic health fanatic who wanted a delivery in a warm pool with flute music and essential oil candles."

Claire smiled. "Well her baby wanted none of that, he was such in a hurry that she gave birth in the hospital car park at three AM. Mother and baby are fine now, so is the father after we gave him some sedation."

Guillaume forced himself to smile, he didn't want to show that something was on his mind. He tried to push back the images of Marie-Ange, his mother, wailing and Christophe, his father, yelling on the phone to a man on the other side of the world.

Claire continued "And there's a patient who's just come in, she's had a bit of spotting and cramps. She looked up her symptoms on the web and she's convinced she has an ectopic pregnancy." Claire paused. "Docteur, you look very pale, anything wrong?"

"Nothing a strong coffee won't be able to fix."

"So what do you want to do about her?"

"I'll see her while I wait for Madame Dussieux to be fully dilated. I'll give her an ultrasound, that should take care of her."

After a long day that saw twelve healthy babies come into the world, Guillaume walked to the Saint-Marcel métro station, immune to the joie de vivre that had spread across the city of light on this warm spring day. For Parisians old enough to remember, it evoked the day everyone was in the streets celebrating the victory over Hitler they had been praying for. The May 68 generation had found an enemy to replace the one their parents had been fighting, chanting "CRS, SS" as they ran to avoid the batons wielded by the men of the *Compagnie Républicaine de Sécurité*, the dreaded riot police, in retaliation for the cobblestones they were throwing. For the present generation, this day was another opportunity to escape their crowded city for equally crowded destinations.

Another advantage of working on a public holiday was that the usual crowd of morose workers had given way to cheerful but less numerous tourists in the métro, laden with bags of souvenirs and the inevitable boxes of *macarons* that they couldn't wait to eat. Groups of Rom children circulated in the carriages, looking for potential victims. Their modus operandi was well known of the police: while one distracted the attention of the unsuspecting commuter by asking him to sign a bogus petition, the other ransacked the contents of his pocket or bag.

Guillaume stopped to listen to a busker at the Bastille interchange. Every day he filled the corridors with the poetry and humour of the songs of Georges Brassens. *Gare au gorille* (Beware of the gorilla), the story of the horny gorilla that escapes and, faced with a choice between a magistrate and an old lady, goes for the man with a robe put a smile on Guillaume's face. The busker was middle-aged, with a beard, a flannelette shirt and worn out jeans. He looked like he was homeless, was he sleeping under a bridge somewhere along the Seine?

"You really know how to sing Brassens," Guillaume said. "You're faithful to the way he sung, I like that. I'm not a fan of the Jazz versions that have come up lately."

"My mother loved him," the busker said. "I grew up listening to his songs but it's only later that I came to understand the messages they contained. *Gare au gorille* denounced the death penalty, that's why it was banned from the radio for three years."

"I thought it was because it was so bawdy."

"That's what the authorities said but it wasn't the real reason. Never believe what they tell you, they're no better now than they were in those days."

Guillaume looked at the busker's eyes. They mirrored the sorrow that was entrenched in his soul—like him, he had lost a loved one. The vibrations of his suffering shook him deep inside.

The busker noticed the frown on his face. "Are you all right?"

"Ah yes, I'm fine thank you." Guillaume said, as the dizziness started to recede.

The busker picked up his guitar to play another of Guillaume's favourite songs *Les copains d'abord*, but Guillaume rushed to the platform to catch the number 1 line. The three stops to his destination, the Saint-Paul station, gave him just enough time to catch his breath and wipe the sweat on his forehead.

Number 5 rue de Sévigné was in the heart of the Marais district. The convenient location made it a very desirable address. It was a five minute walk to l'université Jussieu where Guillaume had studied, and ten minutes by métro to l'hôpital de Pitié-Salpétrière. Louis, Guillaume's grandfather, a retired wine merchant who had properties in several regions of France, had bought an apartment in this building which had been meticulously maintained since its construction in 1904. Bénédicte had lived there while she was studying, and when it had been Guillaume's turn, he had accepted Louis' offer.

Guillaume entered the code and pushed open the wrought iron and glass door. Madame Rimaldi, the concierge, smiled when she saw Guillaume. She had been a concierge all her working life and didn't imagine herself retired; she would miss her loge, the small apartment that came with the job. Its strategic location on the ground floor allowed her to monitor all coming and goings of the building and the street, an entertainment she didn't weary of.

"*Bonjour* Docteur Chambon, I see you were working today. What a pity, it was such a beautiful day. Come in, I've made some gelato for you."

She knew his weakness for home-made gelato. It gave her the opportunity to share the news of the residents' lives that she had collected, and give him an update on her ailments.

Guillaume glanced at his watch. "Thank you very much Madame Rimaldi, but I'll have some another time. I have an urgent phone call to make."

The lift was out of order since this morning, no doubt it was too expensive to call a repairer on a public holiday. Guillaume sighed and walked up the four flights of stairs to his apartment.

The *belle époque* style, with its wooden panels and warm colours, made the apartment a fitting home for his antique clock collection. They were in every room, except his flatmate's bedroom.

Sylvie had grown up like Guillaume in Gevrey-Saint-André, a little village in the Côtes de Nuits region of Burgundy, famous for its prized *Grand Cru* wines. But it wasn't home for her anymore. Home is where you feel loved as you are, and she knew she would be rejected if she came out. Everyone in the village knew where Guillaume was living, but only Sylvie knew that the Marais had become the gay district of Paris. When she had asked him if he had a room to let, Guillaume had hesitated at first. One of the bedrooms was empty, but she was ten years younger than him and he didn't know her. His father had persuaded him to accept—she was the daughter of his parents' friends, the Fayets, and they would feel reassured if their daughter wasn't left to her own devices in the big city. Welcoming Sylvie was a decision he did not regret; she filled the apartment with her liveliness and their friendship had grown over the years. Her small height, pointy nose and spiked hair, dyed purple that week, had earned her the nickname of 'Pixie'.

Guillaume didn't wait for her to drink an aperitif like he usually did when he knew that she was eating at home. He needed something to soothe his nerves. He took a bottle of white wine from the fridge and poured himself a glass. He sat on the sofa and looked at his latest acquisition. A nineteenth century English astronomical clock he had bought the previous week on a trip to London was placed on the marble mantel piece. Its three dials gave the time, the phases of the moon, the date in the form of a perpetual calendar and the orbits of the moon and the six planets known at the time. Clocks were a reminder that time was the only dimension that man could measure but not travel in. Except the past paid regular visits to Guillaume and rekindled the hurt.

As he thought about the births he had assisted today, his eyes caught his sister's painting of the Buddhist wheel of life. It represented the constant cycle of life, death and rebirth. He remembered the meaning of the Sanskrit characters written in orange.

Death is the true companion of birth and never far behind, it is part of our nature.

Does the candle shed a tear when the flame goes out? Don't be sad, be mindful.

Death, the opponent in the battle that doctors fought every day. They knew that it was only a matter of time before it won, but his specialisation was the furthest from death, it was a celebration of life.

Bénédicte had embraced the faith of her husband, and it had comforted her after her best friend Natacha died in a car accident. There were days when the wisdom of the painting's message gave Guillaume strength, but today was not one of them. A day of life and death, he thought as he remembered the day his world had fallen apart. Just when he had got used to the idea that his beloved sister was on the other side of the world and that he was going to be a long distance uncle, life had asked him to accept that he would never see her again.

Guillaume loosened the collar of his shirt and poured himself a second glass.

Sylvie walked in the room and sat next to Guillaume; she knew what this date meant to him. "How was your day?"

"Not as bad as I thought, until I spoke to a busker in the métro."

"What sort of songs does he do? Oh, sorry, I interrupted you."

Guillaume was used to it, Sylvie was as spontaneous as she was sensitive.

"He does really good covers of Brassens, probably not your cup of tea. Anyway, I saw in his eyes that he had lost someone close to him, and his sorrow collided with mine. It was overwhelming."

"How could you tell that just by looking at his eyes?"

"I don't know. There are lots of people who've lost a husband, a sister or a child, but it's the first time I've seen it in someone's eyes."

"Did he say anything about it?"

"No and I didn't ask him; he doesn't look like the type of man who would confide in a stranger anyway. He has to put on an act to look jovial, otherwise he would end up starving with an empty hat. The songs he sings are funny too. I love that Gorilla song."

"Clowns can be the saddest human beings—do you know how many comedians are on anti-depressants?"

"No, I must say I don't have time to keep up with the problems of celebrities."

"There are more than you think."

"I'm surprised they tell anyone, I thought they were so attached to their image. Or did an indiscreet pharmacist sell the information to *Voici*?"

"Well there's one actor that spoke about his experience, it's Pierre Blanc. He had a depression and he said that there are too many people who don't get treated because of the stigma that's attached to mental illness. You know, the usual reaction is 'Just shake yourself out of it'."

"Yes, we've done a lot of education in the hospital about post-partum depression, but it's harder for men to seek treatment. And when they do, they find that it doesn't make the problem go away. Sure it helps you to get through the day, but that's all." Guillaume swallowed, trying to repress his emotions.

"I'm sorry Guillaume, I didn't mean to—"

"No don't be sorry. I'm really grateful to have a shoulder to cry on. My parents have built a wall of silence around my sister's death, they don't even talk to each other about it."

"You've done a lot for me too, you've always been there for me and it's thanks to you I can be myself here. I was suffocating in Gevrey, what a hole!"

"You know, sometimes I feel her presence. I don't know if it's because she lived here or if she's communicating across a parallel universe where she married a *Bourguignon*."

"And lived happily ever after, do you really think so? Look I know it's hard for you to hear this, but you've told me how passionate she was about what she was doing. She really believed she could make a difference, and now that's what you want to do too, isn't it?"

"Yes, it is."

It was his sister's death that had led him to his choice of profession. He had thought about Bénédicte's dream, to help lift Laotian children out of poverty by giving them an education. The world was filled with injustice and she had wanted to make it a better place. That she hadn't been given time to fulfil her dream was an injustice in itself. But he had found something he could do to redeem her death and make a difference himself. He recalled his mother's reaction when he had shared his plan with her after he had finished his fourth year at high school.

"Bénédicte shouldn't have died, it could have been avoided," he had said. "I'm going to be an obstetrician so that wherever I'll be, babies will enter this world landing safely in their mother's arms. Giving birth should be about life, not death, but look at all the countries where it's not the case. I'm going to practice a few years in France and then join Doctors Without Borders."

His mother hadn't greeted the news with the enthusiasm he had expected. "It's not going to bring her back, is it? What if they send you to a war zone? You're my only child now, I can't afford to lose you as well. When Bénédicte said she was going to give birth during the wet season, I had a bad premonition. I asked her how she was going to reach the hospital, but she told me not to worry, there were women in the village who could help her give birth at home. And now you're putting your life in danger."

But there was no stopping him. He had decided to follow the path he had drawn, no matter what.

A well laid plan, but isn't it well known that when men make plans, God laughs?

Chapter Two

13th May, Saint-Joseph church, Dijon.

"None of us will forget Louis, what he did for his family and for the winemakers of the Côte de Nuits. He will live in our hearts for ever." Christophe paused and looked at the mourners that had filled the church. Louis' fellow members of the *Confrérie des Chevaliers du Tastevin* (Brotherhood of the Knights of the Wine-Tasting Cup) were recognisable by their crimson and gold robes symbolising the red and white wines of Burgundy. Louis had risen to the rank of *Commandeur* and had asked to be buried in his robe, with his silver tasting cup and ribbon. His death, on the 8th of May, had been unexpected. The last time Christophe had seen his father-in-law, one week ago, he was his usual self. Marie-Ange had made him a *coq au vin* and he had asked for seconds, washed down with Christophe's wine which he never failed to praise eloquently.

"He had a way of making you feel special," Christophe continued. "When Marie-Ange introduced me to my future father-in-law, I'd prepared myself to make a good impression. I needn't have bothered. He welcomed me in his family without any reservations. He was enchanted that his daughter was marrying an alchemist of the grape. That's what he called the winemakers. He used to say that they transformed the humble fruit of the vine into an elixir of happiness to be enjoyed by everyone.

He believed that good wines could do more for world peace than all the diplomats put together. He often said that after drinking a Côte de Nuits, no one wanted to make war because it soothed your body and your soul and made you sing and thank the lord for blessing Burgundy with His goodness. When Japan liberalised the import of wines, he was the first one to introduce the French produce to the Japanese. He stayed in Tokyo for longer than his family liked, but it was for a good cause. He ran wine connoisseur classes where the only wines sampled were from Burgundy. He told his students that King Louis XIV's physician recommended that he drink only wines from Nuits-Saint-Georges for their health giving properties. They were happy to drink wines fit for a king, and it made us happy too."

Smiles lit up the assembly, as the mourners remembered Louis' sense of humour.

"Louis, you believed that the shortest way to paradise was the stairway to the cellar, and I hope that you have found your way to the great cellar in the sky."

Guillaume had often heard his mother complaining that her father had never been there for her. He was always on the road, promoting the wines of the region and his family had no say in the matter. She suspected him of using his charisma for other purposes than selling bottles of *Grand Cru* wines. Her mother changed the subject every time she brought it up, but Marie-Ange thought that she forgave him when he came back from his trips with gifts and poems he had written in her honour.

Lucky Mum's half brothers and sisters haven't been invited to the funeral, there wouldn't be enough room for all of them here.

Guillaume loved his grandfather and how he had made him travel when he recounted his trips. His stories were embellished and little details were magnified, but it didn't matter. They sounded real and he made you feel like you had been there with him, living the same adventures. Guillaume's path was not going to take him to the same countries. Most of those where Louis had sold wines had a high standard of living and weren't in need of humanitarian organisations like Doctors Without Borders.

Tears for his grandfather mingled with those for his sister and the loss he had never accepted. His father had explained that she was going to be cremated at dawn the next day and that her ashes were going to be scattered on the Mekong River. The first available flight to Laos would have arrived one day after the cremation.

He clenched his hand and his nails bit into his palm.

Why couldn't they have waited, or sent her body or her ashes back to Gevrey-Saint-André?

Bénédicte's family-in-law, like all Buddhists, believed that cremation symbolised the liberation of the soul of the departed from the illusion of the material world. It was meant to ensure a speedy voyage of the soul in seeking a new life after death, and delaying it would have been a bad omen for her and her family.

That was the explanation that Keona had given. Guillaume hadn't understood it at the time and today, it didn't make any more sense to him.

The books he had read on the subject of grieving hadn't helped him. They said that relatives can never get closure when the body hasn't been recovered. There was nothing he could do but continue to live, but every funeral he went to brought back questions that he had buried in the deepest part of his mind.

How can we be sure Bénédicte died? We never saw her body, not even her ashes. All we have is a phone call giving us no details. If only we had been able to give her a proper funeral like this one. If only she hadn't met Pathana...

Guillaume shivered. Sylvie took his hand. A comforting touch, understanding eyes, ears that could listen to his hurt.

He whispered to her, "Thanks for coming Sylvie. I really appreciate your presence, although when the villagers see us together, it's going to get tongues wagging again."

"Not as much as if they knew the truth. I keep putting off telling my parents, I know it will break their heart. But the longer I wait, the harder it's going to get."

When the speeches had finished, the priest continued the ceremony and Guillaume thought about Louis' views on religion. He believed in God but didn't agree with the church's view on sins. "It's a sin to live your life without enjoying what the Lord has so kindly provided us," he often said. "Enjoy today as much as you can. Who knows, tomorrow you may not be here anymore and you will have missed out. I'm not a hypocrite like those bigots who go to mass and then vote for the Front National. They're so scared of going to hell that they live miserable lives. If they had their way, it would be hell on earth."

Louis was right, it was well known that churchgoers made up a sizeable proportion of the members of the extreme-right party and Sylvie had every reason to feel uncomfortable here. She was safer in Paris, where support for the Front National was the weakest and where the openly gay mayor, Bertrand Delanoe, had been re-elected in 2008.

Guillaume was dreading the reception; Louis had wanted to be remembered for what he loved, good wine, good food and good company and wine was going to flow freely. Guillaume wasn't in the mood for singing the customary *Chevaliers de la table ronde* (Knights of the Round Table), with its dubious moral about drinking before you die.

On the other side of the globe, the news of Louis' passing had come to the attention of the Master of the temple that was hidden in the jungle. He hadn't needed to read the funeral notice; he had seen the ceremony as clearly as he saw his students ready to listen to his message. They were dressed like him, in a purple robe. He had chosen that colour to distinguish his order from other Buddhists. It was the only touch of colour in the austere temple; he believed that images and effigies of Buddha distracted from the study of sacred scriptures and the meditation that led to enlightenment. He wore a gold necklace with a cross-shaped purple crystal; it gave him the ability to see what a person was seeing and feel what a person was feeling by concentrating on his name, no matter where he was.

"The custodian of the Vidhi-Vikalpaka has left this plane of existence," the Master said. "The time we have been waiting for approaches when it will be brought back by his descendant and the cosmic order will be saved from destruction."

"Master, may I ask a question?" a disciple asked.

The Master nodded.

"If he discovers its powers, he could misuse it. Or someone else could take it from him. What would happen then?"

"You have many questions for which the answers were written long ago. I saw that these things could happen, for the three persons who are attracted to the Vidhi-Vikalpaka are comparable to the three creatures of the wheel of life. Their actions are predictable, but if they stray I will give put them back in the right direction."

"What if one of them found enlightenment—wouldn't he break free from the wheel of life?"

The Master glowered. "Do you think it can be found on the ground, like a coin someone would have dropped?"

The disciple dropped his chin to his chest and replied with a weak voice. "No Master, it is fruit of discipline, study and exercises."

The Master considered his disciples. They were thirsty for the knowledge he dispensed. It was food for their mind, but they would have to work harder to transform it into wisdom. Only then would they be ready to be handed over one of the sacred crystals. He looked at Analu; young and keen to learn, he reminded him of his younger self. He was one of the three privileged disciples that had a crystal, and he had proved himself worthy of that honour.

"Analu, what can you tell me about the three creatures of the wheel of life?"

"They represent the three poisons that are the root causes of all suffering, Master. Everything that causes us dissatisfaction, pain or suffering stems from one of these three elements. The cockerel is greed, the snake is hatred and the pig delusion. They feed off each other. A lack of understanding leads to craving that can never be satisfied, inevitably leading to anger and hatred." He paused and closed his eyes. "I have seen the one who is governed by the pig. His knowledge of the human body overwhelms his mind and makes him confused about everything else. He doesn't have the awareness to see his ignorance. But his lack of understanding will be beneficial to the achievement of your plan."

The Master acknowledged his answer with a slight bow of his head and closed his eyes to end the discussion. A bell rang three times to signal that it was time to study the sacred scriptures.

A week later, all the formalities had been completed; Guillaume was now the owner of the apartment where he was living and Marie-Ange had inherited Louis' house. After his wife had passed away two years ago, Marie-Ange had tried to convince him to move in with her, but he couldn't see himself living anywhere else than his big empty house. She had asked Guillaume to help clear it with Christophe before she put it on sale.

"You can take all the stuff he brought back from his trips," she said in the van Christophe had hired. "They remind me of his absences. He used to bring us souvenirs, but I never kept them."

"Are you sure you've got all the keys?"

"The front door, back door, letter box, what else would there be?"

"No padlock keys?"

"No, why do you ask?"

"Just in case we found something inside that was locked."

"Ah, you're thinking about that trunk again, aren't you? Well, you can have it, I don't care what's in it."

Guillaume smiled as he remembered the tale he had made up as a boy about the mysterious trunk in the attic.

There must be a treasure in there, maybe something he stole from the Japanese emperor. That's why it's locked and he doesn't want to tell us what's in there. It would be safer if it was buried. The emperor will want it back and send his Samurai troops with their big swords and ugly masks. If they torture us, I won't say anything, I can stand the pain.

He had filled his notebooks with stories of fantasy kingdoms. The last one he had written was about a king's nephew who kills the prince in his crib and caught in the act by the queen, kills her as well. He had stopped writing after Bénédicte's disappearance and he had burnt the manuscript.

He remembered the smell of the smoke, the feel of the warm ashes in his hands. A part of him had died and he had scattered its ashes in a little creek. He had watched them carried away by the clear water on a long journey, first to the river Saône, joining the Rhône at Lyon and then finishing in the Mediterranean Sea. Bénédicte's ashes had been carried by the Mekong River into the South China Sea. The endless cycle of water fascinated him. An evaporated drop of water made its way onto a cloud that could carry it for hundreds of kilometres, and why not to the other side of the world? He liked to think that the rain that fell on his father's vineyard contained water from the Mekong. If that was true, there were molecules of water that had carried the ashes of his sister in the wine that his father made.

Guillaume's musing was interrupted when they arrived at the house, located in the Montchapet district of Dijon, home to the town's wealthy merchants. Marie-Ange opened the gate and Christophe drove in; the tyres screeched on the gravel. The shadow of a five storey building covered the house; Louis had sold the plot of land at the back of the house, knowing he would never have time to look after the orchard that covered it, to the dismay of his grand-children who had enjoyed playing there.

Guillaume and his parents braced themselves; they had fifty years of accumulated paraphernalia to sort. The furniture and valuables were going to be auctioned, and the rest was going to be donated to charity. They worked their way through the house, starting from the ground and up to the second floor where the four bedrooms of his children still had beds for his guests.

Guillaume rescued a secretaire and a Comtoise clock from the auction. The longcase clock was typical of those that were made in the Franche-Comté region in the nineteenth century, with a curved potbellied case and an ornamented pendulum bob that extended up the case. It would look perfect in his living room.

He hesitated about a painting of the desert that looked like it had been made by an amateur. The initials MR were on the back of the frame rather than on the painting. Guillaume went through the names of his relatives, but no one he knew had those initials. *It could be a modern art painting*, he thought as he put it with the other ones.

Guillaume climbed in the attic; it had been a refuge from the world of adults where he and his cousins played, while parents and grandparents were discussing politics and other boring subjects. The metallic trunk had stayed in the same corner, dust from the years gathering on top. It looked ordinary, Guillaume had thought no one could have suspected its presence, a perfect hiding place for a treasure. Now he was starting to have second thoughts.

What if it contains love letters from his myriad of mistresses? I don't want to know the details of his sleazy past. I suppose I could have a quick look inside and if that's what it is, I'll destroy them. No one needs to know Louis' secrets, they are safe with me.

He lifted the trunk; it was too heavy to contain only paper. He was going to have to wait; there wasn't anything in the house that could cut the lock.

Guillaume drove back to Paris in the van the next day and his neighbour, Monsieur Taillefer, helped him to carry the trunk and the clock to his apartment, under the watchful eye of Madame Rimaldi.

He tried cutting the lock of the trunk with a metal saw, but it was tougher than he thought. He gave up after ten minutes, the saw had hardly made a dent in it. He turned his attention to the secretaire.

I'll ask Gilles to confirm but it looks like Empire style, early 1800's, beautiful oak wood. He pulled out the two sliders that were used to support the desktop and looked through the nooks and drawers.

A key turned in the front door. Sylvie shouted, "Guillaume, I'm home. What treasures have you brought back from your grandpa's house?"

"Sylvie, come and have a look at this beautiful piece of furniture."

"It's nice. Was there anything interesting inside?"

"I found his diary."

"Have you read it?"

"No, I haven't had time yet. I know most of the stories anyway. Except those about his affairs, but I don't know whether he's confessed all his sins to his diary."

Sylvie looked at the trunk. "And what's in there?"

"It's a mystery for the moment, I can't open that lock."

"Use a blow torch, that's what they use in bank jobs when they don't want to make too much noise."

"Sounds dangerous." Guillaume paused. "Any other ideas?"

"You're no fun, I was looking forward to a bit of excitement. Did you look everywhere for the key? Maybe it's hidden under a rock in the garden."

"We did a good job of cleaning the house, not so much the garden though."

Guillaume turned to the secretaire and pulled on one of the drawers.

"I just remembered about that one, it's stuck."

"Haven't you noticed the knob? It's different to the others."

"So? Maybe it broke and he replaced it with what he had."

"Let me have a look."

Guillaume stepped back and Sylvie looked at the drawer from different angles. She grasped the knob with her thumb and index and turned it like a dial. It made a clicking sound.

"Aha, a combination lock, very clever. All you need to do is find the code. Try the obvious ones first, when was he born?"

"I didn't know it until he passed away. It's the fourteenth of April 1925."

The clicking sound continued, Sylvie held her breath.

"It must be something else, another important date. How about his wedding?"

"I don't think it was that important to him. It could have something to do with one of his mistresses, but who knows how many he had."

"What about wine? He loved it more than anyone."

Guillaume's face beamed. "That's it! A vintage year. 1974 was his favourite. It was so precious, he hardly drank it. I found quite a few bottles in the cellar. It seems too obvious, but it's worth trying."

This time it worked. Sylvie yelled "Bingo" and opened it. She snatched the key that was inside and handed it to Guillaume.

"Sylvie, you've saved the day!"

Guillaume inserted the key in the lock, hoping that it would be the right one. It took three attempts before it was released. The hinges of the trunk creaked as he opened it. He had expected anything but what he found inside. It was a typewriter unlike any he had seen before. The round keys were ivory white with golden ornate letters in a seemingly random order.

S U T H C I N R Q Z Y A W E D M B V X F L K P O J G

The platen and the type bars were also golden, and an inscription was engraved above the keyboard, with an infinity symbol inside a circle on each side.

The two friends were speechless. Guillaume put the machine on the secretaire, and they examined it, until the silence was broken by Sylvie.

"Caveat Emendator. What does that mean?"

"It's Latin for Corrector Beware."

"That's weird. It must be worth a lot if your grandpa protected it so carefully."

"Yes, but he had a lot of other valuable stuff in his house, and none of it was locked away. Wherever he went he bought works of art, and he liked to show them because he said they had been created to be enjoyed."

"So there must be something extra special about this one. Do you know where he found it?"

"No, he changed the subject every time I asked him about the trunk. It looks like an antique though."

"I love a good mystery, this is exciting!" Sylvie took her laptop and sat down on the leather sofa. "I'll Google typewriters and see if this one comes up."

Guillaume pressed on the first key and nothing happened. He pressed harder and tried the other keys, with the same result.

"None of the keys work, but there must be a way to unlock it. I can't imagine someone making this as a decoration." Guillaume lifted to look underneath and on the sides. "There's a square hole at the back, but it doesn't look like a keyhole. Have you found anything?"

"Nothing that even remotely looks like it. But I did find some interesting information."

Guillaume sat next to her and looked at the screen.

"Look at this one with its flowery decorations, it's beautiful. It was the first one to use the QWERTY keyboard. It was invented to stop the type bars from getting stuck."

"Very interesting, but that doesn't help us."

"But if all the typewriters made after that one used the QWERTY keyboard, it must have been made before."

"Yes but that was in America; the maker of this typewriter could have been unaware of what was happening over there. Have you found anything on a typewriter with a SUTHCI keyboard?"

"Nothing. This is must be a unique piece that no one knows about."

"No one on the web you mean."

"But everyone and everything is on the web, even old stuff. Look, there's a virtual typewriter museum, let's email them and see if they've heard of it.

Guillaume shook his head. "Not now, I prefer we keep it to ourselves."

Sylvie walked to the fridge. "All this excitement has made me famished. Hmm, not much in here. I'm going to the Macdo, what do you fancy?"

It had been his turn to fill up the fridge but he had had other things on his mind. Guillaume smiled as he remembered his grandfather going to Millau to help the *Confédération Paysanne*, a farmer's union, dismantle a McDonald's restaurant. It had been a reaction to the US restrictions on the importation of Roquefort cheese, and more importantly for Louis, a protest against the rubbish they pass off as food that he wouldn't give to a pig.

"A salad will do."

Sylvie left and Guillaume went back to the typewriter to try an idea he just had. He pressed the letters of Caveat Emendator one after the other, but nothing happened.

After all, it's beautiful enough to be a decorative piece. It looks nice on the secretaire; I'll just leave it there.

Guillaume woke up and looked at the time. It was three thirty. He was hungry, the salad had not been enough to satiate him. He found some biscuits and sat on the sofa to eat them.

A soft hum and an orange light caught his attention. He got up and sat next to the secretaire. The light was coming from the keys of the typewriter. It became brighter and brighter, forcing him to close his eyes. He no longer felt his body and his head was spinning. His fingers began typing.

His name was Hervé Rochard. He was born in 1972 and lived in Boulogne-Billancourt. When he was ten, his father died in a car accident. Two years later, his mother, Mireille, married Alex, a customer of the boulangerie. When he lost his job at the Renault factory, he started drinking and became violent.

"You're a fat cow and your son is a stupid degenerate," Alex said. "He cries every time I raise my voice. Look at him, the useless wimp. I've had enough of him."

Hervé watched his mother begging Alex to leave him alone and receiving the blows intended for him. It was his fault if his mother was suffering; he would rather be dead than be a burden.

Later that year, the police came to take Alex away. Hervé overheard one of the policemen explaining to his mother that the neighbours had heard her screaming and had alerted them.

Hervé went to see the psychiatrist that the social worker had recommended. He prescribed pills that made him feel better and sent him to music therapy sessions where Hervé discovered a world of harmony.

He asked the high school music teacher to teach him to play the guitar and gained self-confidence as he made progress in a varied repertoire. Classical, folk, popular music, he wanted to try everything. His biggest reward was the smile on his mother's face as he played and sang the songs of Dassin, Cabrel and Brassens that she loved.

He worked hard at school to make up for the time he had lost; he wanted to make his mother feel proud. I'm not a useless wimp any more, he thought.

Twelve years later, he married Véronique, a waitress at the Duc de Gascogne, a restaurant where the partners of the law firm where he worked as a lawyer had taken him to lunch.

"Hervé, I'm so happy," Mireille said. "I would never have thought my dreams would come true."

"It's thanks to you Mum," Hervé said, "you worked hard to pay my studies, I'll never forget that."

"Your happiness is my reward. When I think of those years of suffering we went through—"

"Don't Mum, we don't need to talk about them, they're behind us, far far away. I have to tell you that I haven't spoken to Véronique about Alex, she only knows that my dad died in a car accident. I just want to forget him and get on with my life with Véronique. I don't want to jinx our good fortune. We're going to start a family soon."

Mireille smiled and took him in her arms.

One year later, Hervé and Véronique consulted a specialist; their attempts to start a family had been unsuccessful.

"The results have come back," the doctor said. "and the diagnosis is not good I'm afraid. You have a cervical cancer. You will need to have chemotherapy, followed by a hysterectomy."

Véronique gasped. "That means I won't be able to have children."

Later that day, Hervé said, "I know it's going to be hard for you, but I don't want to lose you."

"But there are alternative therapies doctors don't talk about. My mother knows a good naturopath, he's treating her arthritis."

Hervé thought there was no harm in trying. "What's his name?"

"Richard Baglio."

Two days later, they were in his cabinet.

"It's excellent timing Madame," the naturopath said, "I've just come back from the Amazon forest and I've made an extraordinary discovery. The local tribes don't suffer from diseases caused by our modern so-called civilised way of life. They have everything they need to maintain their health. When I went there, the shaman initiated me to his secrets and one of them was Acabamca, a rare plant that can restore the balance of the cells in the body. Believe me, it works and you can be cured without losing your most precious treasure. You will be able to give life. I must warn you though, it is very expensive. But can you put a price on your health?"

"Money is not a problem," Hervé said. "We've saved to buy an apartment, but what's the use of owning our home if it's empty of life?"

He stopped typing and took his head in his hands.
"Guillaume, are you all right?" Sylvie asked.
Guillaume struggled to answer.

"I heard a strange noise and I got up," Sylvie continued. "It was like little bells playing a melody and it was coming from the typewriter. There was light coming from the keys, turning on and off as you were typing. But you couldn't see me. It was like you were under a trance. I tried calling you but you couldn't hear me either. So I just watched you typing until you stopped."

Guillaume blinked and gripped the secretaire with both hands to steady himself. He was silent for a moment and then said, "I saw this man's life flashing before my eyes and I could feel what he was feeling. It was very painful, he had such a hard life: losing his father, getting beaten by his stepfather, then his life turned around and—"

"Can I read it?"

Guillaume gave her the sheets. "It's strange, but I have the impression he's familiar. I don't know where from though. I didn't have any friends at school called Hervé and I'm not acquainted with any lawyers, thank God."

Sylvie looked up from the page she was reading. "Why's that?"

"I mean, in my work. So far I haven't had the need for one, touch wood." He put his hand on the secretaire. "Or maybe his wife?" He continued searching his memory. "No, I don't remember having her as a patient."

"So you think this story is real?"

"Yes, it feels like I've been presented with a medical case, but I don't understand how or why. It's irrational, but I can't ignore it. If they listen to that quack and take his miracle plant, they'll be ruined and it will be too late to save her."

"What are you going to do?"

"Call the gynaecologists in town and ask them if they have a patient called Véronique who has been diagnosed with cervical cancer."

"And then what? How are you going to persuade her to get a proper treatment? You're not her doctor."

"I'll figure that out when I'll find her."

He looked at the Comtoise clock. "Five AM, it's too late to go back to sleep now, but it's too early to call anyone."

"How about a coffee?"

"That would be lovely. Sylvie, you're an angel"

She blushed and turned her head so he couldn't notice.

"How did it go?" Sylvie asked as Guillaume came home from work later that day.

"I was lucky, I got a message from Docteur Lanier. He's very good, I remember him from a lecture he gave at an obstetrics conference last year."

"What did he say?"

"He remembered Véronique, she was his patient six years ago. The last time he saw her, she was very reluctant to consider a chemo treatment. He assumed she had gone to consult someone else to get a second opinion. It happens frequently, so he wasn't surprised. He knew any other doctor would give her the same answer."

"So this story is true then!"

"Yes, but I thought that it was in the present and that I could do something. There's little chance she's still alive now. That bastard! How many women did he kill with his plant?"

Sylvie opened her laptop and started clicking.

"I'll look up the funeral notices to be sure."

Guillaume stood behind Sylvie, looking at the screen. His jaw was clenched and he was rubbing his fingers together. There were fifteen search results, but only one where Hervé's name was mentioned, and it was dated 11th December 2006.

"That means it's the spirit of Véronique that used the typewriter to communicate with you," Sylvie said.

"But hang on, it was Hervé's life that was flashing before me not Véronique's and he never spoke to her about his stepfather."

"Maybe he's dead too. He could've committed suicide after she died. I'll do a search of the funeral notices with Hervé Rochard."

Sylvie scrolled through the results.

"There are a few after 2006 but the deceased are much older than he would have been."

"I've got a feeling he's still alive and there's a connection between us."

"You mean like telepathy?"

"I've never believed in it, but it would explain why I saw his life in such details. It's more plausible than channelling anyway. I mean, once you're dead, that's it. You're gone for ever."

Sylvie typed Hervé's name in the yellow pages web site.

"No lawyer by the name of Hervé Rochard."

Guillaume walked to the secretaire and looked at the sheets he had typed.

"Why didn't the typewriter show me the rest of the story? There's a gap of six years between the last sentence and now."

He sat down and closed his eyes.

"Nothing's coming," he said after waiting five minutes.

"Do you remember if something triggered you to start typing?"

"I got up during the night and saw the light coming from the keys. It was so strong I closed my eyes and then I started typing."

"Looks like you'll have to wait for the middle of the night."

"I'm on call so I may not be here."

"I can watch it. This is exciting, I want to find out what happened."

Guillaume wasn't convinced this would work, but when his friend had decided something, you couldn't talk her out of it.

After coming back from a delivery of a 3.8 kilo baby girl to a demanding American woman, he found Sylvie in a state of excitement. The letters of the inscription on the typewriter,

CAVEAT EMENDATOR, were drawn with a green light on the ceiling.

"I closed my eyes but nothing happened. You try it."

Guillaume did as he was told, with the same result.

"I didn't see those letters on the ceiling last time." He scratched his head. "Corrector beware. But beware of what?"

"There's only one way of finding out. It's asking you to correct the story."

"What do you mean?"

"You've got to make it right. You said that if Véronique took that miracle plant, they would be ruined and it would be too late to save her."

"So what can I do? If that's what happened, it can't be changed."

"What if the typewriter allowed you to write a different course of events? If she went back to Docteur Lanier, could he save her?"

"Well, it's an early diagnosis. I would say she has more than a ninety per cent chance of surviving."

"So just write that Véronique made an appointment with Docteur Lanier."

"What good would that do?"

"What have you got to lose?"

Guillaume tried, but none of the keys worked. "You see, it won't let me."

"She was really determined to go ahead with the naturopath's remedy. What if you found a way to make her change her mind?"

"How can I do that? The naturopath convinced them that she could be cured and still be able to have children."

Sylvie became animated "What if they found out the truth about the naturopath, they wouldn't have a choice, would they?"

Guillaume's eyes narrowed; he was quiet for a moment and then raised his eyebrows. "I think I have an idea."

The keys started to glow, as if the typewriter had picked up his idea, and he started typing, Sylvie standing behind him.

Hervé switched on the TV to watch the eight PM news report, as he always did. It was part of his job to keep up with current events. The headline of the day was an earthquake of magnitude six on the Richter scale hitting Central Java. The casualties were estimated at six thousand, and one and a half million people were homeless. Hervé pricked up his ears when he heard the name of the naturopath who had sold them a remedy for Véronique's cancer. He had been arrested for deceitful conduct and illegal practice of medicine. His stockpile of capsules had been seized and analysed; they were extracts of Valerian, a common plant used to treat anxiety and insomnia. Docteur Lanier was interviewed, saying that if any patients had consulted this charlatan, they should make an appointment with their GP or specialist urgently so that they could get proper treatment without any delays.

Hervé repeated to Véronique what he had heard. "If he hadn't been arrested, we would have continued with his treatment and then it would have been too late. No wonder you've been feeling relaxed and sleeping like a baby. I'm going to make an appointment tomorrow morning to see Docteur Lanier. Don't worry about not having children, we can adopt and you'll be a wonderful mother."

A screeching sound filled the room for a brief moment; it was followed by a slight tremor.

"What was that?" Sylvie rushed to the window and opened the shutters to look outside. She went back to Guillaume. The keys no longer glowed, and the room was silent, apart from the usual ticking of the clocks.

Guillaume rubbed his temples. "Ooh, that really hurt. Just after I typed the last word, I had this searing pain in my head, and I heard this awful noise."

"Yeah, I heard it too, and I felt the room shaking; I thought something had hit the building, but everything looked normal outside."

"I'm glad it wasn't just me."

"What you typed was brilliant."

"As soon as I came up with the idea, I saw it happening with all the details. I was typing what I was seeing like the first part, only this time I was in control."

"Well done, you've saved a life, possibly two."

"Only on paper though."

"But what if it did happen the way you wrote it?"

"But it didn't. The past is the past, it can't be changed. All I did was write how I would have preferred things to happen. We've both seen Véronique's funeral notice, and what I wrote isn't going to bring her back. Now I can't explain why I saw the first part of the story and then I was given the chance to make up a different continuation. Maybe it was invented by an author with writer's block. It's fantastic, it gives you the start of a story and then lets you finish it."

"Hardly enough to write a novel though."

"Well it certainly needs improvement."

"What about the inscription on the ceiling?"

"As well as being a writer, the inventor was also a good handyman."

Sylvie frowned. "You have answers for everything, don't you?"

Guillaume got up. "No, I'm just trying to make sense of a completely irrational situation. Now if you'll excuse me, I've had enough of this, I'm off to bed!"

Sylvie had never seen her friend upset like that, He was usually calm and collected. It's what made him a good obstetrician. He had to put up with patients screaming in agony, sometimes hurling abuse at him and the medical team. When she had asked him why he couldn't give them an epidural to keep them quiet, he had said that sometimes it was too late or there was a religious or medical contraindication. He had explained that it wasn't the best choice because the woman couldn't feel the contractions.

Sylvie was too excited to sleep; she had some work to catch up on. The typewriter had taken her mind off her job; she worked as a graphic designer for the BVP advertising agency and she was due to present her drawings to an energy company. She had imagined Eolia, a fairy who blew the wind that generated clean energy. It had made her girlfriend Clémentine upset because it was the same company responsible for the biggest oil spill of the century. "They're getting a good public image and a clean conscience thanks to your work, you're a traitor!" were her last words to Sylvie. That was ten days ago and Clémentine hadn't replied to any of Sylvie's messages. She loved her job and didn't mind who her clients were. She cared about the environment, but she had different opinions about how the problems could be fixed. Besides, if she had refused this contract, someone else would have taken it and these clients were influential, they could have damaged her reputation. As she looked at her work on her computer, she wondered if they were going to like it, they were known to be unpredictable and her colleague Rosalie had been reduced to tears after a meeting with them. Eolia looked like she was happy and carefree, everything Sylvie wanted to be, and could be if one thing in her life was modified.

I want my life to change so badly that I believed the typewriter could fix it. I have to get back to reality, instead of believing in magic.

Chapter Three

1st June, Tel Aviv, Israel.

Dear Miriam,

As you read this epistle, I am no longer in this world. I have lived a wonderful life, enjoying the delights that it offered me. Sweet Miriam, you have always been in my heart. You had your reasons for not answering my letters, but I hope that we will meet again in heaven so that you can answer this one. As I write this missive, I am looking at your beautiful painting of the Dead Sea. I dream that I am bathing in it and that you are next to me, just like that time at Ein Bokek. I have wonderful memories of—

Miriam put down the letter that Louis had written shortly before passing away. He had given instructions to the notary to send it to her. It stirred painful memories in her heart. At the time, she was minister of Foreign affairs and was looking for a supplier of fine wines for the receptions she was renowned for. He had insisted that she tasted the wines herself rather than her secretary. Curse those wines! They had made her lose her head, or was it his declaration of everlasting love?

She remembered the last time she had seen him. It was in a hotel in Montmartre. He had said that it would be more romantic to spend time with her in the city of love. In fact, it was because it was the only way to keep their affair secret, far from his family and acquaintances in Dijon.

He had spoken about an object he had found in his travels that could change the fate of humanity; a typewriter that could alter events that had happened in the past. She had found it hard to believe, but her anger at his betrayal had made her forget about it.

It all came back now, but did it really matter? If such an object did exist, it wasn't of any use to her, her life was nearly over. But could it change the fate of her people? What if it could erase Hitler from history? She had been saved by a French family, but her parents hadn't been so lucky and had perished, like the rest of her family.

I'm an old woman and I'm thinking crazy thoughts. A typewriter that can change history, it's impossible! My mind has weakened, I'm going to have Alzheimer's if I continue like that. Aaron is coming this afternoon, I better tell him about his father before it's too late.

"Aaron, I have something to tell you," Miriam said.

He leant towards her to hear what she was saying in her soft voice.

"Yes, Mum."

"I hope you forgive me for not telling you this before. I know it's something that is important to you. You have the right to know where you came from. I have been very selfish, thinking only about myself and my bruised ego. Every time you asked me, I told you I didn't want to talk about him, that it was best for you if you didn't know. It must have been hard for you to think that your father was a real bastard, as I used to call him. You gave up asking and never brought up the subject again. I didn't even think about the hurt I caused you."

She paused as his face hardened. It was too late to stop now, she had to continue.

"He was a handsome French wine merchant who sold the most exquisite wines. I thought he was the man of my life, but it turns out he was married and had a family. I was so upset, I never told him about you. Now that he's passed away, I wonder if it was the right thing to do. I wanted you to avoid being rejected as I had been. The truth is, he never stopped loving me and before passing away, he reminded me of his love. He had a big heart, and there was room for me as well as his own wife and family. I don't know how long I have left to live but I wanted you to know I'm sorry before it's too late."

He stayed silent, waiting for his mother to tell him more. It was hard for her, but he was in no hurry.

"If you're upset at me, you have every reason to be. My only hope is that you forgive me before I go."

Aaron remained silent.

"There's something else I ought to tell you. Now bear with me, this is going to sound absurd. I'm not sure if I believe it myself. Your father found a machine that can change events that happened in the past. He claimed that he used it once, and when he saw what it had done, he hid it in a trunk by fear of what would happen if it fell in the wrong hands. I have no proof of this, only his words. The only reason I'm telling you this is to ask you a question: what if this is true? Do you realise what this means for our people? You have the means to find it, what have you got to lose? At worst, if you try it and it doesn't work, you'll have spent a few days of your life trying to put things right. Life is short Aaron. Think of this as my last request."

She closed her eyes, exhausted. Aaron took her hand in his and squeezed it softly. He let it go and went to the bathroom. He splashed his face with cold water and looked at his image in the mirror. Green eyes, a straight narrow nose, a round face, he didn't look like his mother. She had always told him that he was handsome. Was she thinking of his father when she was saying that? He tried to imagine what he looked like when he was his age. He had pushed thoughts of his father to the farthest corner of his mind when he was a teenager and they had stayed there. He had deluded himself into thinking it had no importance, but if he had known his father's name, what would he have done? His mother was right, if he had tried to reach him, he would have been rejected—he was a living reminder of his father's forbidden passion. He had a family that didn't know his existence. How many half brothers and sisters did he have? He never had siblings, his mother had stayed single. She had been forced to resign when her bump became apparent and she had moved to Tel-Aviv, away from the disgrace he had brought onto her.

Is that what I am, the son of an immoral man and a gullible woman? No, I was right, it doesn't matter. I've risen above that, I have built my own life without the help of anyone. It's just as well I didn't know, ignorance is freedom.

He didn't know what to think about his mother's idea. If such a thing existed, it could change the destiny of the Jewish people. But was it another of his father's lies? Mossad, the Israeli Secret Service where he worked, hadn't assigned him yet to a new mission, he could take some leave and travel to France. He loved this country. He had gone a few times with his mother, she liked visiting her guardian angels, as she called them. She was the only woman in his life that counted; he couldn't deny her this small request, even if it turned out to be a wild goose chase.

He came back to his mother and used a wet face washer to refresh her face. She opened her eyes and smiled at him.

"Mum, I will go to France and find out if what my father said about this typewriter is true," he said.

"My beautiful boy, I knew I could count on you."

Guillaume woke up and looked at the clock; It was three AM. The girl he had met last night at the Montgolfière bar was still sleeping in his bed, naked. He had been troubled by something he had seen in her eyes, and he had avoided looking at her eyes for the rest of the night. He had had other things on his mind, like the way she had pretended to ignore him while she was dancing. Now it came back to him, it was the sorrow of having lost her mother when she was a little girl. He didn't understand how he knew that by looking at her eyes; she hadn't mentioned it and he didn't intend to ask her, he didn't want to get emotionally involved.

The whisky he had drunk made him thirsty. He went to the fridge to get a bottle of orange juice, and as he walked past the secretaire, he saw that the keys of the typewriter were glowing.

Oh no, not again! He grabbed Sylvie's jumper from the sofa to put it over the typewriter but as he approached it, he lost his resolve. He was mesmerised by the orange light of the keys and could not resist their attraction. He felt like a piece of metal pulled by a magnet. He closed his eyes and typed what he saw.

Her name was Sophie Lambert; she was seven years old and lived with her mother Armelle in Belleville. She had never known her father, her parents were eighteen when she was born, and he had run away from the responsibility of raising a child. Her grandparents had kicked their daughter out of their house when she had refused to give up her baby for adoption.

The leaky one room apartment in the attic was furnished with the bare minimum: a table, three motley chairs, a black and white television and two mattresses on the floor. Sophie was eating her breakfast, a slice of bread thinly spread with margarine.

"Honey after I pick you up from school," Armelle said "I have to go out for an appointment. It's for a job I found in the paper."

"What sort of job?" Sophie asked.

"It's to look after an old man during the night. If I get this job, you'll have to be brave my sweetheart; I'm sure you'll be able to call me there if anything happens. I've looked everywhere, it's the only way I can earn some money so that we can have a better life."

Sophie repressed her tears, she didn't want her mum to be worried. Armelle turned up the volume of the radio; the news were on—Lady Diana had been killed in an accident. She wiped a tear from her face and hugged her daughter before taking her to school.

The lights of the keys went off. Guillaume stopped typing and opened his eyes. The house was silent, Sylvie hadn't been woken up. The landing back to reality had been smoother this time. He yawned and stroked his chin.

It wasn't a medical case, but he had a feeling this story wasn't going to have a happy ending. There was something that was familiar but he couldn't put his finger on it. What was special about a single mum looking for a job in Belleville? Maybe she wasn't going to get it and would end up on the street, losing the care of her daughter. That would make her heartless parents happy. What else could happen? She was living in a run-down apartment, it could catch fire and they would both perish. He didn't know which year this happened, unless... What year was Lady Diana killed? 1997, the year he passed his Baccalauréat.

He opened his laptop and typed 'Belleville 1997' in the search bar. The first result was a news article: 'Belleville butcher arrested.' Of course, now he remembered! The murderer who lured his victims with advertisements for a job to look after his father during the night. His favourite victims were young single women who had run away from their family. Vulnerable women who were desperately trying to avoid living on the streets, but whom no one would miss. He disposed of the corpses in his coal furnace. The police had taken months to identify his victims, conducting DNA tests on the traces of blood found on his knives and chopping boards and on the floor of the cellar. Guillaume kept reading the article.

> The first identified victim was Armelle Lambert, a single mother aged 26. A neighbour had knocked on the door of her apartment after hearing Armelle's daughter Sophie cry during the night. She was taken to the hospital and treated for shock. The girl told the police her mother had gone for a job interview and hadn't come back. The police found an advertisement she had circled with a red pen and traced the owner of the telephone number. After the police searched his house, making some gruesome discoveries, André Fillon was arrested and is currently in custody.

It looks like I've been given another tragic story to correct, but what has that one got to do with me? The only way to save her mother would be to stop her from applying for that job, but how? Ah yes, I know. The hospital is always complaining they have trouble finding cleaning personnel to work on the night shift. It must have been the same back in those days.

Guillaume didn't have to wait long before CAVEAT EMENDATOR appeared on the ceiling, signalling that he could continue the story he had been given.

That afternoon, Sophie came home from school crying. The teacher had asked the class what the children wanted to be when they grew up and they had answered 'teacher', 'vet', 'hairdresser', 'fireman' or 'cosmonaut'. Except her. She had no idea what she wanted to be. She only knew that she didn't want to end up like her mother. It made her sad to see her mother afraid all the time of not being able to afford the necessities. It was her fault, if only there was one less mouth to feed...

"Honey don't cry, you've got plenty of time to figure out what you're going to be. Look at the way you look after your dolls, I'm sure you'll make a wonderful nurse or even a doctor. But whatever you choose, I'm sure you'll be good at it. You're really clever, you were the first one in the class to read a whole book."

Sophie read the newspaper after her mother had finished looking at the job advertisements. That day there was a section on medical careers that she had skipped. Sophie read the articles and didn't understand everything, but that didn't stop her from imagining herself as a nurse, looking after patients and comforting them. She would see them getting better and thanking her as they left the hospital. Look at all those jobs, I can't wait to be old enough to work so I can help Maman, she thought. She skipped the ambulance driver vacancies and on the last page saw an advertisement that could suit her mother.

"Maman, look, I found something for you. There's a hospital looking for cleaning ladies on night shifts. It says 'No qualifications required and staff benefits provided.' What does that mean?"

"I'm not sure darling. Maybe there's a canteen, or they have a Christmas party and Santa brings presents to all the children."

"Oh please Maman, apply for this one. I don't want you to work at that old man's place. I'm scared."

"Scared of what?"

"Something might happen to you."

"He's an old man, he's not going to harm me."

Tears were streaming her face. "But if he's mean, he'll make you work even you're sick. If you work at the hospital, they'll look after you."

"All right, I'll give it a try."

"Promise you won't go to that old man's house. I'll pray that you get this job."

Armelle smiled. "Yes my angel, I promise. You're so sweet, I don't want you to worry about me. Everything will be fine, I'll get that job at the hospital and I'll be able to pick you up from school every day."

Sophie smiled and took her doll. "Maman look, Nathalie fell and she hurt her knee, she needs a bandage."

Guillaume had forgotten about the headache, the screeching noise and the tremor, but they happened again. He let out a deep sigh. He had saved another life, even if it was only on paper. Life-threatening situations were not everyday occurrences in his job. There had been cases where haemorrhages put mothers' lives in danger, but he had saved them by acting quickly and accurately. His hospital had an excellent track record, no maternal deaths had been recorded since 1995.

He thought about Sophie's dream to become a nurse. The articles she had read conveniently left out the reason for the shortage of nurses in France. They worked long hours, had responsibilities for an increasing number of patients and were poorly paid. The average career length was five years. After that time, only the toughest survived, the others were burnt out. But it had given Sophie hope that she could live a meaningful and useful life when she grew up.

Guillaume went to the bathroom to relieve himself and returned to his empty bed.

"So what did you think of last night?" Sylvie asked the next morning. She was the bass guitar player in the all-girl rock band The Wild Ones. The first time Guillaume had gone to a gig was as a gesture of support, but he had found himself dancing with the rest of the crowd and had become a regular.

"It's strange, I only remember the first half of your gig. That new song of yours is great."

"Which one? We played three new ones."

"Wild about you."

"I'm glad you liked it. What about our cover of Barracuda?"

"Well that's the thing. I don't remember anything after Honky Tonk women. All I remember is waking up and typing another story at three AM."

"And nothing in between?"

"No, but I dreamt that after that song, I left with a beautiful brunette. I'm sure it was a dream. I woke up and the bed was empty. It didn't look like I'd come back with a girl and we'd—"

"You're right, it was a dream, you were there until the end and you looked like you had a bit too much to drink."

Guillaume frowned, searching his mind for a lost part of his memory. "This has never happened to me before, I must be getting old."

"You said you got up to type a story, let me have a look."

Sylvie lit a cigarette and took the sheets, both Guillaume and her forgetting the unwritten rule that smoking was restricted to the balcony. After she had finished reading, she said, "Is that how you recruit cleaning ladies for your hospital now?"

"Hardly, this happened fifteen years ago. In real life, she did go to look after that old man and ended up cut up in little pieces and incinerated. I found the story on the Figaro web site. She was the first victim they identified."

Sylvie winced. "That's horrible. But you changed the story and she didn't go. If it happened the way you wrote it and she got the job, she's still alive!"

"Don't start that again, it's like the last time. I saw someone's life through some sort of telepathic transmission triggered by the typewriter, I typed what I saw, I found out what happened afterwards and I imagined it differently. It gave me good conscience, full stop." Guillaume took his laptop. "We can settle this once and for all. I'll go to my

45

browser's history and I'll prove to you that the butcher of Belleville did kill Armelle."

Guillaume brought up the article and Sylvie read it.

"I can't see any mention of Armelle Lambert being a victim," Sylvie said.

"Let me see." Guillaume hit the refresh button and read the article again, slowly. "It must be the wrong page." He trawled through the history and made more searches. "I can't find it anymore, that's impossible. I remember it clearly, it wasn't a dream. I looked it up after I wrote the first part of the story. If it hadn't been there, I wouldn't have written the second part."

"Yes and now it's still there, except Sophie's mother is not in it anymore because you stopped her from going to that butcher's place. If that's not enough proof for you, open the white pages and look for Sophie Lambert."

There was no person by that name.

"Sophie's twenty-two now, but she could still be living with her mother, unless she's married. Try Armelle Lambert."

"Four of them. What are you going to do, ring them and ask them if they applied for a cleaning job at the hospital fifteen years ago?" Guillaume asked.

"Why not?"

"If you have nothing better to do."

"Unlike you, I believe there are things that science cannot explain."

"Well if a typewriter that can change history existed, don't you think it would be known?"

"Maybe that's because your grandfather hid it so well."

Guillaume shrugged. "I have to go to work now, good luck with your phone calls, you can tell me all about it tonight."

The discussion with Sylvie hadn't given him time to eat breakfast; he bought a croissant at the *boulangerie* on the way to the métro.

What a rotten start to the day, none of this makes any sense. If the typewriter caused as many problems for Louis, no wonder he locked it up. I think that's what I'll have to do. Or maybe throw it to the bottom of the Seine so no one else has to endure this.

At the Bastille interchange, a violinist was playing. According to the sign, he was a student at the conservatory. Guillaume stopped and dropped a two-euro coin in his violin case.

He thought about Joshua Bell, the world famous violinist who had played at a Washington metro station for an hour on his Stradivarius and only one person recognised that a virtuoso was playing.

Guillaume walked past this spot every day; it was strange that he had no recollection of anyone playing here, whereas he remembered others, like the clarinet player at the saint-Paul station. The memory of a dream where he stopped here to speak to a middle-aged man playing the songs of Brassens came back to him. He had been moved by the sorrow of having lost a loved one he had seen in his eyes.

"Are you a regular here?" Guillaume asked the young man.

"No, there's usually a woman who sings Edith Piaf songs, but she's gone to see her sister. She found her after she appeared on that TV show where they look for long lost relatives."

"Have you seen a busker playing Brassens in this part of the métro?" Guillaume asked another busker.

"No, but if you're looking for one, you could go to the space in front of the Georges Pompidou art museum where Dédé is playing."

Could these memory blanks be a symptom of Alzheimer's disease? There have been early cases, as young as thirty. I'll make an appointment with a specialist tomorrow.

Madame Riondel, Guillaume's first patient of the say, was expecting her third child and had come for the first ultrasound.

"And how are Rémi and Antoine?" Guillaume asked.

"Fine, fine."

"And now a little number three, let's see how he's going. Please lie down here."

The woman wasn't her usual self. She nodded, but didn't move.

"Is anything wrong Madame?"

"I forgot to take my pill one day, I swear it was an accident. I put off telling my husband I was pregnant until yesterday, he was furious. He said I had to choose between him and the baby. I don't want to lose him, what am I going to do on my own? I really wanted to have a big family, it was my dream. I had four brothers and sisters and we were so happy together." Guillaume gave her a tissue and she wiped a tear. "He said that he didn't want to see me coming back from the hospital still pregnant. He's asking me to commit murder on an innocent life."

Guillaume had seen it many times, a woman who wanted a bigger family forgetting to take her pill. But abortion wasn't a means of contraception and he had the right to refuse. There was a conscience clause in the abortion law that allowed him to do so and he always did. His speciality was about bringing new lives into the world, not destroying them. He believed in the original Hippocratic Oath which prohibited abortions, but the government had conveniently revised it. His hospital was within the national average, one abortion for every four births and his colleagues complained about the additional work Guillaume's refusals gave them. He did make an exception if the woman or the child's life was in danger, but she wasn't in that case.

"Madame, I know it's a very difficult situation for you, but have you tried discussing this with your husband? You don't want to rush this decision."

"Docteur, you didn't see the look on his face, I'm scared just thinking about it!"

What does she expect from me? I'm not a marriage counsellor.

"But surely you could negotiate. I mean, if he's worried about the financial burden, you could remind him of the very generous allowance for the third child. Or what about going through with the pregnancy and giving him up for adoption? There are a lot of parents on the waiting list, your child could make a childless couple happy."

"I could never abandon my child, it would be a betrayal and I would regret it for the rest of my life. No, I know it's wrong, but if I have to choose between two evils, I would rather go through with it now."

"I'm sorry, I don't practice abortions but there are other doctors here who do. I can recommend Docteur Goury, he's very good."

Madame Riondel took Guillaume's hand. "But I don't want to see another doctor, you're the only one I trust. Please, Docteur Chambon, it's hard enough as it is."

She looked at him anxiously, waiting for his response.

She trusts me, I can't let her down. I don't want to do this anymore than she does, but it will be more painful for her than for me.

"Tell your husband that there is a one week delay, it's the law." Guillaume handed her a form. "Here's the paperwork, you can show it to him if he doesn't believe you. I will see you next week, unless you can make him change his mind."

"Thank you for your understanding Docteur."

Madame Riondel left just as Guillaume was being called to delivery room number four.

"Madame Grenelle, 32 years old, first pregnancy," the midwife said. Contractions started an hour ago, but cervix is already dilated to ten centimetres. The husband is on his way"

49

"Thanks Jocelyne." Guillaume turned to the woman. "Bonjour Madame. I'm afraid we won't have time for an epidural. Everything is going well, it will be over in no time."

But as he spoke, he saw in her eyes that she was living her last minutes. He could not see why, everything looked normal. A few minutes later, she was having trouble breathing and the monitor showed her blood pressure dropping. Docteur Perrin, a doctor from the emergency ward was called to assist. He inserted an endotracheal tube to assist her breathing. When her heart stopped beating, he administered an electric shock with the defibrillator to get it started. It wasn't enough. After increasing the power to three hundred produced no result, he asked the nurse to inject one milligram of adrenaline.

One problem solved, another emerged. The woman's body shivered and she started bleeding abundantly. The student nurse who was on her first day of work experience fainted, but the team's attention was focussed on saving the young woman.

"The blood is clotting, get some plasma and platelets," Docteur Perrin said.

"We have to save the baby, I'm going to perform a C section. Fabienne, get me a scalpel," Guillaume said.

He had performed dozens of caesareans before and his actions were precise. But he didn't think of it as a routine procedure, nothing was—every delivery was different. He put thoughts of the mother aside while he was delivering the baby, it was his role to save him.

The sound of the monitor beeping as the mother's heart stopped was drowned by the cries of the baby. Life versus death, it was a draw.

Docteur Perrin made another attempt to save Madame Grenelle; while Guillaume was stitching up her abdomen, sixty milligrams of amiodarone were administered with the infusion pump to stimulate her heart, but it was too late.

Guillaume suspected that his patient had suffered an amniotic fluid embolism, a rare complication that occurs when amniotic fluid, foetal cells or hair enter the blood system of a pregnant woman via tears in the uterus or cervix during labour and trigger an allergic reaction. The autopsy was going to confirm this.

A counsellor had been called to support the father who had been kept out of the obstetric theatre. Guillaume turned off his pager and walked out of the hospital. He sat down on a bench in the gardens, deep in thought.

How could this happen here in Paris, this isn't Darfur! I have a professional team, the best equipment, everything to protect women's lives when they give birth. Why did this have to happen? Why didn't I do something when I saw that she was in danger?

He thought about everything he and his team had done, reviewing every move to find a possible mistake or omission. He was oblivious to the cold wind and the rain. His mind drifted to the typewriter as he imagined himself typing the story and changing its conclusion. He got up abruptly.

I'm a doctor, I'm responsible for my patients. It's my duty. No one can change what's happened. I'm supposed to be strong, not the one who needs counselling.

As he came back, Claire looked at him with equal doses of concern and reproach.

"Docteur, where were you? We're waiting for you, it's time for your round."

Life continued, it had no time for the dead and those who lived in the past.

When Guillaume came home, he went straight for the sofa; he looked at the typewriter. He hoped that Sylvie's attempts to contact Sophie's mother had failed. It would prove that it was only a conduit for telepathic transmissions. He could accept that, but using it to change the past was going too far. He hadn't seen anything like it in the science-fiction novels he read in his teenage years. Time travel was often mentioned, but this was different. You didn't have to travel, the past came to you and then you altered the events from the comfort of your chair. Like you were God, watching from a distance and pulling some strings to make things as you wished them to be. Only it didn't work like that, even God didn't have that power. Otherwise, why would he let millions of people be slaughtered, or die in natural disasters?

Sylvie burst in the living room. "Guillaume, guess what! My clients loved Eolia, they just want a few minor changes and then they'll start using her in their advertising."

"Yeah, great."

"Try and show a bit more enthusiasm!" She looked at him sprawled on the sofa. "Tired from last night?"

He recounted the day's events, while Sylvie got herself a beer from the fridge.

"I know it must be hard for you, but I'm sure you did your best."

"I keep asking myself whether I did, but I can't see where I made a mistake."

"That's probably because you didn't. Relax, you're not God, these things happen, you can't control everything." She gulped a mouthful of beer. "I have other news which I'm sure you'll find interesting."

Guillaume sat up and looked at her, expectantly.

"The second Armelle Lambert I called hesitated before replying that she had worked in a hospital. I could feel in her voice that she was surprised about my question. Obviously she didn't trust me and I don't blame her. When I asked if she had a daughter called Sophie, she said it was none of my business and hung up."

"That doesn't prove anything."

"What more do you want? Look at the facts. You've stopped Armelle Lambert from getting cut up by a serial killer by finding her a job in a hospital, and now she's still alive and well in Ménilmontant."

"It could be another Armelle Lambert."

Sylvie threw her hands up. "You're hard to convince, but I'm sure that one day something will turn up that you can't refute."

Sylvie had to be careful what she wished for, that day was closer than she thought, and it was going to affect her life in a way that she could never have imagined.

Chapter Four

20th June, Paris.

Intrigued by the typewriter, Guillaume took it to Gilles' antique shop at the place des Vosges. Gilles had become not only Guillaume's favourite supplier, but also a close friend. His wealth of knowledge about the history of France amazed Guillaume. His small shop was specialised in rare pieces and Guillaume was the first to know whenever Gilles found a clock. He had come across one of the rare ten-hour clocks that had been made during the short period in the French revolution when France had adopted decimal time, but it had been too expensive for Guillaume. He opened the door slowly and the smell of linseed oil reminded him that the secretaire could do with a polish.

"*Bonjour* Gilles, I wanted to get your opinion on this typewriter." Guillaume put it on Gilles' desk.

Gilled examined it. "What an amazing piece, I've never seen anything like it. Where did you get it?"

"It was in my grandfather's attic, but I don't know where he found it."

"I'm sure it has an interesting story to tell."

Guillaume didn't say anything; he trusted Gilles, but the least he or anyone else knew about the stories the typewriter could tell, the better.

"And the keyboard, look at those characters," he continued, "the workmanship is flawless, the ivory is top grade, and the type bars are solid gold. It's exquisite! But why make a typewriter so beautiful? It's fit for a king! Not that I imagine a king typing, of course. When they have anything to write, they just dictate it." He pressed the keys one after the other. "The only problem is, it doesn't work. And the keyboard layout is unique. SUTHCI, that reminds me of something, but what?"

Gilles removed his glasses and chewed the ends as he searched his mind. He was a man who had no need for Internet, everything was stored in his memory.

"Ah yes, I remember! The holy church of Suthci, an obscure sect that was founded in the 1870s. They were based in the little village of Chantenay-sur-Loire, near Nantes. They believed that Jesus Christ was an extra-terrestrial being who used his power to perform miracles, and who went back to his planet on the day of the ascension. The name of their church comes from ICHTHUS, the ancient Greek word for fish, which is also an acronym for 'Jesus Christ, God's Son, Saviour'. They kept a low profile, but when the villagers found out about their beliefs, they burned down their house of worship because they thought they were Satanists. There was no record of any survivors. I wonder if they have anything to do with this."

"But where did they find the typewriter, and what did they use it for?"

"It's only a hypothesis, and it's going to be difficult to confirm it. Very little is known about the members of this sect, apart from the founder Émile Vattier. He was an inventor and a friend of Jules Verne. He could have made it himself." He paused and put his glasses on his head. "There is one thing you could do."

"What's that?"

"Get it carbon dated. The base is made of wood and the keys are made of ivory, both are organic and allow carbon dating. I have a friend at the Jussieu University. He's an archaeologist and has helped me in the past. It would give you an approximate date. At least you would know when it was made. I can also ask another friend at the patents office. He could search the archives to see if Émile deposited a patent for this typewriter."

"Thanks Gilles."

As he was about to leave, Guillaume saw in Gilles' eyes that a fatal disease was starting to develop in his body, but he could not see where. He could not ignore it after what happened to Madame Grenelle.

"Gilles, how have you been feeling lately?"

"Same as always, rather good."

"You haven't been more tired than usual, or had any pain?"

"No, not really, why? Have you seen something I haven't, Docteur Chambon?"

"Um, no, but at your age I really think you should get a complete check-up; it's fully covered, you won't have to pay anything. I don't want to alarm you, but even though you're feeling fine, there could be something lurking in your body that the check-up will uncover."

Gilles' voice dropped. "You're not thinking about cancer are you?"

"It's always a possibility, but the check-up will give you peace of mind. It will only take an hour of your time."

Gilles cleared his throat. "I'll take your advice, better be safe than sorry."

The next morning, when Guillaume went to the kitchen to eat breakfast, he found Sylvie was already up, spreading Nutella on a slice of fresh baguette. They were lucky to have what was considered by many the best *boulangerie* in the district two minutes' walk from their apartment. Whoever got up first, if they had time, had the duty of buying bread and of leaving some, if they could, for the other.

"Hi Sylvie, you're up early," he said.

"Yeah, we're rehearsing for the *fête de la musique* this morning"

"Are you playing at place de l'Hôtel de Ville again this year?"

Tonight was the twentieth anniversary of the free music festival, where all types of music were played in all sorts of places. When Guillaume had looked after the pregnancy of the Paris public space occupation officer three years ago, he had put in a word for Sylvie's band which was just starting. She had allocated The Wild Ones a slot in a prime location, and it had helped the band to get some paying gigs in the city's venues.

"You've done a good job, Madame Plessy's still looking after us; we're making the most of it while it lasts. She could give our slot to another band whenever she wants." She looked at Guillaume. "You look like you've had a rough night."

"I couldn't sleep, I've got an appointment with the administrator this morning; his secretary didn't say anything, but I bet it's about the investigation on my patient's death."

"I thought it was going well; you said your colleagues had assured you that there was nothing you could have done to change the outcome."

"The investigators may have a different opinion on that."

"There's no point being stressed out in advance though. I'm sure you'll be fine." She took the baguette and said, "Don't go on an empty stomach, I'll make you a Nutella tartine."

Guillaume smiled; Sylvie looked after him like his mother did—it was her maternal instinct, he thought, although she had said to him that she was 'light years' away from being ready to have children, and in any case she would let her partner bear the first one. If that was the case, she would not have legal custody, the law hadn't caught up with reality yet, and French lesbian couples had to go to Belgium, the closest country where they had access to In Vitro Fertilisation.

He ate the tartine Sylvie had prepared, washed it down with an espresso and went to the hospital, where he arrived ten minutes before his appointment. He went directly to the administrator's office where, to his surprise, the secretary let him in straightaway.

"Bonjour Docteur Chambon," Charles Bondel said. He was due to retire in two months, after a long career in the Paris public hospitals. He had been administrator at l'hôpital de Pitié-Salpétrière for the past ten years but it was the first time the two men met. "Make yourself comfortable, I'll get coffees brought over."

Docteur Patrick Renouil walked in the room and barely acknowledged Guillaume. An ambitious surgeon, he had been selected to be Charles' successor and had started to make plans to increase the efficiency of the hospital wards.

"So you're the man who has tarnished our reputation of the safest maternity hospital in Ile-de-France, well done." He looked at Guillaume with hard, cold eyes.

"But I followed the protocols and—"

Charles raised his hand to stop him. "Let me put it another way. It was unfortunate that this patient chose our hospital, that's all. I have read the report of the investigation. The conclusion is clear, there was no human error or omission. Amniotic Fluid Embolism is a rare condition that can't be prevented. Docteur Chambon saved the child and I have been informed by the paediatric unit that he is in perfect health. It could have been much worse had he not acted so swiftly and efficiently."

Charles paused to let his words produce the expected result. Guillaume relaxed, while Patrick took the news as a disappointing setback to his plan to replace the obstetrician. Charles' secretary put a tray with three coffees on the desk. The three men took their cups and started sipping the strong black liquid.

"That's what I call coffee," Guillaume said. He had never got used to the stuff that was served in the staff cafeteria.

"Now there is another matter that has come to my attention," Charles said.

The two men put their cup down and looked at Charles expectantly.

"Do you remember Amanda Drysen?"

"Yes, it's not often we get American women, they usually prefer private hospitals. The delivery went very smoothly, the baby was healthy," Guillaume said.

"Yes, apart from one minor but important detail." Charles paused to emphasize his point. "You forgot a gauze pad in her most intimate area. She has had a thorough examination performed by an independent specialist. It confirmed that it didn't get infected or cause any damage. That's the good news. The bad news is she's suing the hospital and asking one hundred thousand euros for emotional distress."

Guillaume was speechless; he was thinking about the repercussions on his career and his prospects of working with Doctors Without Borders. Would they still accept him?

"One hundred thousand euros? That's way over the top!" Patrick said.

"That will be up to the judge to decide. Unless Docteur Chambon chooses an out of court settlement."

Patrick turned to Guillaume. "Out of your own pocket of course. The hospital doesn't have money to waste."

"That woman must have friends in high places, the hearing is in two weeks. These procedures usually take months." Charles said. He ended the conversation and showed Guillaume out of his office.

On the day of the hearing, Guillaume walked the three hundred metres from his apartment to the *Tribunal Administratif*. He had gone to the hairdresser the day before and wore his best suit. A few shops were closed for the holidays. France was divided into two camps, *Juilletistes* who took their holidays in July and *Aoûtiens* who preferred August. Both ignored the advice to avoid leaving or returning on the week-ends, and faced hours of traffic jams to get out of Paris and onto the *autoroutes* that would take them to their destinations to the south or the west. For those who had the misfortune of staying, the city council transformed the banks of the Seine into 'Paris-beach' with sand, umbrellas and ice-cream vendors.

Guillaume looked at his watch and wiped his forehead. It was stifling inside the old building. Hot summers were the norm since the 2003 heat wave that had killed fifteen thousand elderly people in France. The country had not been prepared for this onslaught, and a refrigerated warehouse at the Rungis wholesale food market had to be used to store the bodies that the funeral parlours had no room for.

Charles, Patrick and Guillaume's lawyer arrived shortly after and exchanged polite greetings with Guillaume. After a two-hour wait during which the four men remained silent, they were called to the court room.

The magistrate was a stern looking woman with short black hair and rectangular glasses with a thick frame. Guillaume, worried, turned to his lawyer who nodded and smiled to him.

"Case number 21589, Mrs Amanda Drysen versus l'hôpital de Pitié-Salpétrière," the court clerk announced. "On the 25th of May of the year 2012, Mrs Drysen was admitted to l'hôpital de Pitié-Salpétrière to give birth to her first child Ava. The obstetrician who assisted the delivery was Docteur Chambon. According to his declaration, he performed an episiotomy on his patient as the baby was large and his shoulders were stuck. This surgical act was designed to give him more room to perform manoeuvres to free the shoulders from the pelvis. Moreover, it was a prophylaxis for preventing severe tears that are difficult to repair. After the delivery, he proceeded to stitch her..." The clerk hesitated to continue.

"That's fine, clerk, you can skip the anatomical details."

The court clerk cleared his throat. "Upon returning to her home, 25 Boulevard de Vaugirard, Mrs Drysen felt her...

ahem ... itching. Upon self-examination, she felt a lump and her husband drove her to the emergency department of l'hôpital Européen Georges-Pompidou. A nurse removed a gauze pad that had been left there by Docteur Chambon. The next day, Mrs Drysen had a thorough examination performed by Docteur Dayard who prescribed further tests. They confirmed that there was no consequence to the gauze pad having remained for a period of five days. During the time between the discovery of the gauze pad and the obtention of the results of the tests, Mrs Drysen suffered considerable anxiety at the thought of not being able to bear another child. She is requesting that the hospital pay an indemnity of one hundred thousand euros for the emotional distress that she suffered."

"I see Mrs Drysen isn't present today."

"That is correct your honour. She is represented by Maître Hervé Rochard."

Guillaume sputtered the water he was drinking. Hervé looked up from the paper he was reading and turned his head to look at him.

"Maître, do you have any observations to make to support your client's request?" the judge asked.

Hervé Rochard widened his eyes and stared at Guillaume.

This isn't looking good, Guillaume thought.

"Maître, we are waiting," the magistrate said. "We are already running behind schedule, so please make your point concisely."

"Your Honour, please accept my apologies for wasting your precious time. My client is hereby dropping all charges against the hospital."

The four men gasped at looked at each other to see if any of them had understood what had just happened. The judge sighed. "Apologies accepted. Clerk, please make a note that this case can be closed and call in the next case."

The four men walked out and Hervé invited Guillaume for a coffee, while Charles and Patrick walked to the métro station to return to the hospital.

"I don't know how to thank you Maître, you have saved my career and I hope yours won't suffer." *And that Mrs Drysen won't find another lawyer to reopen the case.* "But why did you do it?"

"To thank you for saving my wife."

"I don't know what you mean."

"My wife had a cervical cancer and I had a dream about what my life would have been like if she had continued to take a remedy that a naturopath had prescribed. At the end of the dream, I saw you with a typewriter, writing that the naturopath had been arrested to stop my wife from continuing to take the plant. When I woke up, I had a symbol tattooed on my hand, the same that's on the typewriter."

Hervé showed this palm to Guillaume.

Guillaume looked at it in disbelief. "Tell me more about your dream," he said to gain a bit of time.

"When my wife's health started to deteriorate, we went to see the naturopath, but he insisted that it was a sign that her body was fighting back the cancer and that she had to continue taking the pills. I spent all my savings to buy them, but her condition continued to degrade. I drove her to the emergency department after she collapsed and the doctor told me that it was too late; her body was completely invaded by cancer cells and she only had two months to live. I held her hand as she passed away at the hospital. Then I saw myself staying at home too depressed to work. I lost my job and I was evicted from my apartment for unpaid rent. I attempted to reunite with the love of my life by jumping into the Seine River, but Bernard, a volunteer from *Restaurants du Coeur* saved me."

Guillaume nodded; he donated regularly to the charity that distributes food to the needy.

Hervé continued. "He convinced me that life was worth living and that my wife would wait for me in heaven. I didn't go back to working as a lawyer though. I used my guitar to earn a few coins from commuters who enjoyed my renditions of Brassens songs. On Victory day, you stopped to speak to me and saw the sorrow in my eyes. The next thing I saw is you writing an alternate course of events on a typewriter, the one that I had lived, where my wife was cured. I read the sheets you had typed and then I woke up. When my wife asked me about the tattoo, I told her about my dream. We prayed to thank God for the life we had with Juliette, our little girl we adopted in Madagascar." He pulled a photo of his daughter out of his wallet. "When I recognised you, I couldn't go through with the case."

Guillaume ran his hands through his hair.

"I wondered if you were God or an angel," Hervé said. "And you know what, I had that dream on the same day that my client gave birth to her daughter. I don't think it's a coincidence, this meeting was meant to happen so I could thank you. But tell me, who exactly are you?"

Guillaume didn't know what to say, he hadn't had time to let the reality sink in. The events he had written had come true, and there was an alternate reality where he had spoken to Hervé at the Bastille interchange. Both Hervé and he had seen it in a dream. That's why he couldn't remember who was playing in the métro, a part of his memory had been erased. *I can't explain to him what I don't understand myself, I shouldn't have accepted to have a coffee with him.*

"I'm sorry to disappoint you Hervé, but it's a coincidence that the man in your dream looks like me. Look, it's true your wife wouldn't have survived if she hadn't had proper treatment. You're lucky that charlatan was arrested and maybe your dream is a message for you to be grateful for what you have. But I have nothing to do with it. I had never seen you or heard of you before today and I don't know your wife either. I have no patients by the name of Véronique Rochard and—"

"But it is you, I'm sure! How else would you know my wife's name?"

He muttered "Oh it was just a guess." He looked at his watch and got up. "Thanks for the coffee. I have to go now, I have an appointment in ten minutes. Goodbye."

"But wait…"

Guillaume rushed outside, leaving Hervé with his questions.

"I knew it! The typewriter can alter the past," Sylvie said after Guillaume had described his encounter with Hervé. "I was going to look at the funeral notices again to convince you, but I don't have to. You changed Hervé and Véronique's lives with the typewriter. If it had stayed in Louis' trunk, Hervé would still be busking and you would walk past him every day without knowing his story."

"But why did the typewriter make me change Hervé's life rather than the life of a man in Iraq who's lost his wife and children because they went to the market when a suicide bomber decided to explode?"

"Because you made a connection with him and not the Iraqi man." She paused and looked through the window, as if she had seen something. "Remember you had a dream about a girl you picked up at the Montgolfière, it must be Sophie. You changed her life, as a result she never went there and you never saw her. That's why you don't remember half of the evening. There was a connection there as well, although of a different nature."

Guillaume played back his dream and the vision the typewriter had given him. Both Sophie and the girl in his dream had green eyes and dark brown hair. An important detail came back to him, the girl's name was Sophie. Why had it taken him so long to make the link?

"So if I understand correctly," Guillaume continued, "this is how it works: first, contact is made between the person and the owner of the typewriter who sees in his eyes that he's lost a loved one. Then the typewriter's keys glow and he views the person's past up to the time before the loss. He types an alternate continuation which changes the past, and his memory of the encounter is erased and replaced by a dream, because the result of the change he made is that it didn't happen. The person has a dream about his alternative life and wakes up with a tattoo on his palm of the symbol on the typewriter."

"The same thing must have happened to Sophie; if she sees you, she'll recognise you."

"I should recognise her as well; I made a big change to her life, but she should look the same. It was different with Hervé; it took me a while to recognise him without his beard and his dirty clothes. Anyway, I don't want to interfere with her life now, I hope she has a boyfriend."

The next day, as Guillaume walked past Madame Rimaldi's apartment, she called him. "Monsieur Chambon here you are, I was waiting for you. Have you given your entry code and your keys to anyone lately?"

"No the only person who has them is Sylvie and she wouldn't give them either. Why?"

"Yesterday I was at the lab for some blood tests that the doctor prescribed because I've been feeling tired and I've lost a bit of weight. I've lost my appetite and that got me worried—"

Guillaume didn't want to spend the rest of the afternoon listening to her health problems. "Oh I'm sorry for you Madame, but what has that got to do with my keys?"

"Well, I didn't have time to clean the hallways yesterday like I usually do on Tuesdays, so I did that today. As I got to your floor, I saw a man come out of your apartment. He said 'Bonjour Madame, nice weather for the season' and walked down the stairs. He seemed distinguished, I didn't dare say anything to him but I thought I better mention it to you just in case."

"What did he look like?"

"Dark hair, about your height, in his fifties. He wore a very nice suit and a Fedora. He had a bit of an accent though."

"What sort of accent?"

"American, I think."

"I don't know anyone who fits that description, but thanks for mentioning it Madame Rimaldi."

"Do you think I should have called the gendarmes?"

"No, you did the right thing, don't worry."

"If there's anything missing, do tell me first, I feel responsible."

"No I assure you, it's all right. But I will check and let you know."

Madame Rimaldi returned to her apartment and made a sign of the cross. Guillaume opened the door of the lift and pressed number five, wondering who that man could be. He didn't fit the profile of a burglar, but how did he get in? He must have known that neither Sylvie nor he were at home at the time. Guillaume opened the door slowly and searched for signs of objects missing, moved or broken. Everything looked as it was when he left this morning.

When Sylvie came back from work, he asked her to check her room. "Madame Rimaldi said that she saw someone walking of the apartment. I haven't found anything missing, but I haven't checked your room. I wouldn't know if there was something wrong in there." Guillaume followed her; clothes, books, CDs and drawings were scattered on her bed and on the floor. "How do you manage to find anything?"

"I know it's messy, but I have a good memory. I know where my stuff is, I don't even have to look for it."

It was more than he could say. If one thing wasn't put exactly where it should be in his well-organised bookshelves and cupboards, he spent more time looking for it than he had spent organising.

"So everything is…" He hesitated to say "in order".

"Yeah, it's all there."

Guillaume found Sylvie's habit of chewing gum irritating but refrained from making a comment. She looked everywhere to see if she could spot an anomaly as they went to the living room.

She gasped. "The typewriter, where is it?"

"I left it with my friend Gilles, he's going to get it carbon dated. It will tell us when it was made. He thinks it may have been invented by the founder of the church of Suthci."

"The church of what?"

"Suthci, you know, like the first letters of the typewriter."

Guillaume repeated what Gilles had told him about the sect; when he had finished, Sylvie said "I don't know about Jesus, but maybe this machine was made on another planet. Its advanced technology is far more advanced than anything on earth."

Guillaume wasn't surprised by Sylvie's reaction. She loved to watch Doctor Who, a British series about an alien humanoid who travelled across time and space in a machine that looked like a police telephone cabin. "I don't know. I used to love science-fiction when I was a teen. I looked at the stars and dreamt of life in other galaxies. I stopped that when I started my studies." Guillaume grinned. "I was too busy thinking about earthlings to worry about how alien females give birth."

"I wonder if there's as much violence on other planets."

"Maybe not, but I don't believe in ideal worlds either, I think it's just part of life wherever it is."

Guillaume noticed that Sylvie squinting and biting her bottom lip. "Are you OK?"

"Yeah, just a bit of migraine. I'm going to lie down and have a rest."

Guillaume's apartment was Sylvie's safe haven and knowing that someone had entered when they were out had triggered a reminiscence of the abuse she had suffered in her childhood. It had left deep scars in her soul, like the scars on her arm she had made with a knife. They too were a reminder that something in her had been destroyed and she would never recover completely. Wounding her skin had helped to relieve her anxiety, but she had stopped when she had fallen in love with Brigitte. She had thought that love would have healed her, but it had only made her wound deeper, for Brigitte was a victim herself. Her father beat her and her mother for no reason. Her mother said that she had fallen in love shortly after he had served a prison sentence. She thought that she could change him, for it wasn't his fault, he had been beaten himself by his father. If you've always known violence it conditions your life, unless you discover love—it has the power to change everything, doesn't it? But the damage was irreversible and she couldn't bring herself to leave him because that would have been a betrayal. Brigitte was angry at her father and her mother for being their victim. She didn't know how to deal with her anger and when it caught her off-guard, she directed it at Sylvie who forgave her, until she realised that she couldn't continue to be the recipient of Brigitte's anger. Ending their relationship had been a painful decision, but she was up against something that couldn't be changed. She didn't want to make the same mistake that Brigitte's mother had made.

Was the man responsible for her pain reproducing what he had suffered himself? It wasn't an excuse, there was no justification for it. A jury would surely agree with that, but she had never told anyone, it would be his word against hers. He had influential friends and would be able to get away with it. The abolition of privileges brought by the French revolution was a theoretical concept. The reality was different. President Chirac was a crook, everyone knew that, but he had got away with fraud and bribery.

She tried to put things in perspective by thinking about the many souls who had suffered worse than her, but it only gave her only relative comfort. She could not remember where she had read that suffering was like gas—if a certain quantity of gas was pumped into an empty chamber, it filled the chamber completely and evenly, no matter how big the chamber. Suffering was the same, it completely filled the mind and the soul, no matter whether the suffering was great or little.

She took a pencil and a drawing pad; she had found that occupying her mind by drawing or writing a song helped her in difficult times, but nothing came. She reached for her Xanax; it was her last resort, she didn't want to be dependent on a drug.

Her phone rang; she looked at the screen, it was Clémentine. She let it ring; she didn't want to get back with her now. She had too much on her mind.

Unbeknownst to Sylvie, four monks had heard her conversation with Guillaume and listened to her thoughts, thanks to a sacred crystal they each had.

"The companion of the doctor is a servant of the cockerel," the Master said. "It represents greed. She does not crave material things, but the excitement of new experiences. She thinks she is finding freedom in her creativity, but on the contrary, by using it to numb her suffering, she is attaching herself to it.

Do not be under the delusion that you have reached enlightenment once and for all. Your body and your mind are constantly changing. The molecules of your body are renewed every seven years. You must reconquer your freedom from the three poisons every day. If you drop your vigilance, they will come back, make no mistake! If the study of scriptures and the meditation give you a pleasant sensation, beware. The greatest poison you face is spiritual lust. It is very devious, it tricks you because the object of your craving is spiritual."

"What are we to do, Master?" a disciple asked.

"Be aware, always. Spiritual lust operates in the dark and the light of awareness weakens it. If you recognise it for what it is, it loses its power. But as soon as you close your eyes, it comes back." The Master knew what he was talking about, he had fallen in the same trap. When he had realised the contradiction of attaching himself to spiritual practices that directed him away from any sort of attachment, he had mastered the techniques that sharpened his awareness.

"And how does the girl fit into the plan?" Anula asked.

"She is useful. She will stop the doctor from ruining it, because her very existence depends on it."

Chapter Five

13th July, Gevrey-Saint-André.

"Something strange happened the other day," Marie-Ange said. "An American man came to buy a few bottles, and he told me that he had met Louis in New Orleans in January 1986. His father had a restaurant in the French Quarter, and Louis had made his father and him taste some Côte de Nuits *Grand Crus* wines. According to him, Louis had tickets to the Super Bowl match the next day and he had invited them to join him. Then he handed me his business card." Marie-Ange gave the card to Guillaume: 'Jeffrey Wheeler, antique dealer'. "He told me that Louis had spoken to him about a rare typewriter, and that he was prepared to give me a good price for it if I had it in my possession. He looked disappointed when I told him I had never seen it before and then he left.

When I mentioned this to my friend Monique who's the mayor's secretary, she told me that she had seen him the day before. He consulted the civil registry, saying that he was researching his genealogy because he had relatives here. He stayed at the hotel des vignerons, and Madame Fiquenlit said that he asked questions about the local families."

"How long ago was this?" Guillaume asked.

"Hmm, about ten days ago. I didn't think too much of it at the time, but then I remembered. Louis had planned to go to New Orleans in 1986 and had booked tickets to the Super Bowl match. It was a really cold year and he slipped on an icy footpath the day before his flight. Your father had to take his place. Oh he was so disappointed, he went on about it for weeks. Your father doesn't remember this man at all. In fact he did go to the match, but it was with some friends of your grandfather. They were officers of the New Orleans *Sous-Commanderie* of the *Confrérie*. Then I thought, maybe he went to New Orleans another year but your father said he didn't."

"What did he look like?"

"Dark hair, moustache, about your height. He wore a Grey pin-striped suit and a Fedora. There was something about him that looked familiar, but I couldn't put my finger on it."

It must be the man who was in my apartment, he was after the typewriter, Guillaume thought. *But how did he know about it? And how did he know that Louis was supposed to go to New-Orleans?*

"What's wrong Guillaume? You look like you've seen a ghost."

"Nothing, I'm wondering who this man is."

"Madame Fiquenlit told me he checked out of his room the next day, and he hasn't come back."

"It's probably nothing to be worried about then."

"By the way, did you see a typewriter when you were sorting his stuff?"

"What? A typewriter? No, no I didn't," Guillaume said hurriedly.

Whoever this man is, he's very clever. It's just as well the typewriter is with Gilles.

"The Fourteenth of July lunch is going to be special this year, it's Alphonse Blancarré's hundredth birthday."

"If I ever live that old, I hope I'll be like as sprightly as him. The last thing I want is to vegetate in a wheelchair. If that happens, I'll ask someone to put me out of my misery."

"But you're a doctor, how can you say that?"

"Because I know my limits; there's only so much that can be done in the face of suffering. Death always has the last word anyway, and we doctors try to delay it because that's our job. But all we're doing is prolonging the agony."

"Guillaume, it's not like you to speak like that, you've always been passionate about your job since you decided to be a doctor. Are you sure you haven't been working too hard?"

Despite his resolution not to bother his parents with his worries, Guillaume spoke about his patient's death and how it had affected him. It reminded them of the capriciousness of life and that their sorrow would be with them until their own passing.

The next day, the villagers were gathered in the village hall for the traditional lunch. French flags were hung on the walls above the paintings that the children of the school had made on the theme of Bastille Day. Antoine was the lucky winner of the competition, and had walked away with a book on the history of France that he had tucked away in his bookcase, never to be seen again.

Escargots drowned in garlic butter were followed by Boeuf Bourguignon cooked with a copious amount of red wine; it was now time for the cake. Henri Fayet, mayor of the village and president of the Burgundy region council cleared his throat loudly and waited for the chatter to dissipate. "It's an honour today to celebrate one hundred years of a life well lived in our village by a man whom we all know and love. Here is a man ready to give his life for us. A valiant and distinguished soldier, a volunteer fireman, always ready to lend a hand, always smiling, a loving father and husband. Let's cheer for Alphonse! Hip, hip, hooray!"

As the villagers sang 'Happy Birthday to you', Alphonse prepared himself to blow the hundred candles on the giant birthday cake baked by Monique and Marie-Ange. He wore a suit adorned with his medals, and a beret. His eyes had the sparkle of a man who loved every minute of his life. After he blew the candles with help from his children, he stood up and raised his glass.

"All this hard work has made me thirsty, let's drink a toast to our beautiful village and its inhabitants."

As he put down his glass of champagne, he looked around him and smiled. "This is my one hundredth celebration of our national day. How convenient to be born on the same day," he chuckled as the guests clapped. "Of course, the first time I wasn't allowed to drink." He paused. "I had to wait the second year." The villagers laughed. "All my Air Force comrades are now drinking from the great barrel in the sky. I will join them when God decides my time is up. I remember the first national day we celebrated together after our country was liberated. Some of you present here were children or young adults and may remember. For the others, let me tell you the story of how we celebrated it in the old days."

The room became silent, Alphonse was renowned as a great story teller and today no one would be disappointed. Guillaume thought about Louis, he was fourteen at the time of Alphonse's tale. He had lived his childhood during the war and appreciated the peace that had lasted until his end. Guillaume's generation took peace for granted, but if Doctors Without Borders sent him to a war zone, he would soon find out first-hand what it was like. What if the typewriter could be used to stop a war from happening? He struggled to imagine the consequences of World War II not happening. War was part of human nature; another war would have erupted in its place and it could have been deadlier. He turned his attention back to Alphonse.

"The day started with a procession from the village hall to the war memorial, led by Lieutenant Raidillon, commander of the firemen corps, followed by the air force, including yours truly, Paul Ledoux the mayor, Father Armand, the school children and the singers from the parish.

Soon the commands rang: on a 'right, right', half of the procession turned to the left." Alphonse paused to look at the smiling faces. "The Lieutenant Raidillon's moustache, although full of authority, shuddered. The order somehow restored, the procession resumed until Raidillon shouted 'Stop, stop, you fools, you forgot the flag at the Town Hall!'

When we finally arrived at the war memorial, the mayor delivered his speech. Then the school children sang the song of departure, and at the same time the parish singers began the Marseillaise, and Popol, the communal police officer full of zeal, blew the first notes of 'At the Flag' with his bugle.

'Stop, stop!' yelled Raidillon. After an impeccable salute, our lieutenant spoke again: 'We will now observe a moment of silence for the dead of the wars of 14-18 and 39-45.'

Then the whole village went into the school yard where a greasy mast was erected, at the top of which were suspended sausages, cakes, candy and tobacco packets. The mayor asked Popol to demonstrate. Quite proud of this honour, he puffed his chest, spat in his hands and grabbed his arms around the mast. Encouraged by the crowd gasping, and with much grunting, swearing and sweating, he finally reached the summit. Upon picking up the package, disaster! Popol slid down the mast and fell on his back side, causing general hilarity." The audience laughed and Alphonse, smiling, took another sip of champagne.

"In the evening, as the municipality couldn't to afford a fireworks display, it held a ball instead in the village hall. The mayor came and opened the ball and we advised Popol to choose his partner; without hesitating, he went straight to his sister-in-law. Now you have to imagine Popol with his 150 centimetres and fifty kilos in the arms of his sister-in-law with her 170 centimetres and hundred kilos, and the centrifugal force gained in the frenzied waltz they were dancing. It made Popol gradually take off the floor. Suddenly, in an uncontrolled skid, Popol crashed to the ground, receiving his sister in law on the chest. Of course, having

Popol as a shock absorber, the sister-in-law was fine." The villagers laughed again.

"Meanwhile Popol was half conscious and it took three glasses of wine before he came to. We evacuated our dear Popol and after being copiously lectured by his wife for having demolished her husband and forgetting his cap, we returned to the ball which ended late at night.

That was one of my most memorable national day celebrations and I hope you enjoy this one."

As the old man sat down to the sound of applause, Henri started singing *Joyeux enfants de la Bourgogne* and everyone joined in the chorus '*Je suis fier d'être un Bourguignon*' (I'm proud to be a Bourguignon).

As Guillaume walked to his parents' house after the lunch, he looked at the vineyards that had made his village renowned. From March to September, winemakers watched over the growth cycle of the grapevines. Starting with the bud break, followed by the flowering, the fertilisation, the fruit set and the veraison (ripening), every step was vital to the development of the grapes.

His preoccupations were similar, he watched every step of the growth of foetuses, until he harvested the fruits of the womb. Fertility problems had become more common, with many women putting off their first pregnancy until they were in their thirties. Here, the proportion of flowers that had been fertilised was higher than the usual fifty per cent. But this was no guarantee of the quality. The harvest was two months away and anything could happen. Winemakers were at the mercy of the weather, vine disease and pests.

The miracle of life renewing itself time after time had always fascinated Guillaume. Nature provided in abundance and yet it was fragile. Man's help was needed and women were not equal. Their chances of giving birth successfully depended on where they were born. Guillaume was proud that one day he was going to play a part in making the world a little bit fairer.

Guillaume heard the sound of thunder. He looked at the sky; there wasn't a single cloud, could it be the air force jets flying to Paris for the Bastille Day parade? He looked down and saw the ground covered with hailstones that had destroyed the grapes. He looked up again, there was still nothing. He shook his head and looked at the vines; they were intact and the hailstones were gone. It was another vision of a loss, but not one that he could remedy. He decided against telling his father; even if did believe him, there was nothing that he could do.

When Guillaume arrived in Paris the next day, he went directly to see Gilles who had left a voicemail saying that he had the results of the carbon dating.

"Look at this exquisite vase I bought this morning," Gilles said. "It was made shortly before the revolution. When I look at the pieces in my shop, I think about the hundreds of years of history they've witnessed. If only they could talk, they would reveal a multitude of joyful and dramatic events. Lives have started and ended in their presence, love has flourished and faded, and crimes have been—"

"You said you had the results of the carbon dating,"

"Yes that's right. You were lucky, my friend just had time to do the carbon dating before his holidays. He's in Sicily now, although I don't know how much of a holiday it is. He never goes anywhere without his tools, just in case he stumbles on something interesting. Sicily has a very interesting history, it has been conquered by a multitude of invaders. Did you know that Roger II the Norman became king of Sicily in 1130? His court became the most luminous centre of culture in the Mediterranean and—"

"What about the typewriter?"

Gilles walked to a table and said, "Here it is, unscathed by its ordeal. The wood and the ivory are dated 1868, give or take a year or two. My friend told me something interesting happened, the keys started glowing. He thought it was strange so he put it through an X-Ray machine to see what was inside. It was the only way, I hope you don't mind."

Guillaume was anxious at the thought that the secret of the typewriter had been revealed, but tried not to show it. "No, that's all right."

"He saw there were some crystals underneath the keys. Very unusual, what could they be used for? And how could they generate light? I must say this has opened up more questions than provided answers. But the main clue that will help us to track its maker is the date, two years before the church of Suthci was founded by Émile Vattier. My friend at the patent office looked through the archives, there were twenty-seven patents lodged by Monsieur Vattier, although it doesn't look like any of them made him rich. No mention of the typewriter though."

Gilles saw the look of disappointment on Guillaume's face. "But I think that trail is still worth pursuing. I mean there are some concordant signs: the year, the keyboard layout. He could have kept it secret for some reason, or if he perished in the fire, he wouldn't have had time to lodge the patent. I did some research on Émile Vattier. He had no descendants, but he had a brother named Léon and I found his great grandson, Marcel."

Guillaume gasped. "You found him? What did he say?"

"When I said I found him, I just meant his name, with the help of a genealogist. But I would be very interested to speak to him, he might be able to confirm that it was his great great uncle's invention."

Guillaume grabbed the typewriter. "I don't think that's necessary. I'm sure he wouldn't know anything. I better go now, I have an appointment."

"Before you go, I wanted to thank you for your advice. The doctor put me through a battery of tests and the results for prostate cancer came back as positive. It's at an early stage and the specialist is confident it can be cured."

"I'm sure you'll be fine Gilles."

After putting the typewriter back on the secretaire, Guillaume opened his laptop to search the white pages. There were several men by the name of Marcel Vattier, but only one in Chantenay-sur-Loire where Émile was born. By the time Sylvie came home, he had already tried several times to call him.

Sylvie was carrying a guitar case. "Look Guillaume, I got myself a new bass guitar. It's a Les Paul, like the one Suzi Quatro played."

She opened the case and showed it to him. He looked at it briefly; he had never heard of Suzi Quatro before he met Sylvie; she was her role model, the first female bass guitar player who headed her own band in the history of rock. Sylvie put the guitar back in its case, but left it open to continue admiring it.

Guillaume repeated to her what Gilles had told him. "I think I've found Monsieur Vattier, but he isn't answering his phone."

He poured himself a glass of wine, but didn't offer one to his friend. She had a small beer bottle in her hand. To those who questioned her preference for beer, she replied that having been brought up in a wine village, she got sick of seeing it and smelling it. Guillaume enjoyed the wines of his village, but didn't subscribe to the commonly held although biased view that French wines were the best in the world. He thought that some Australian and Californian winemakers beat the French at their own game, but avoided saying so by fear of being branded a heretic.

"Even if his great great uncle did invent the typewriter, do you think he knows anything about it? It was made a long time before he was born."

"His grandfather may have talked about it or about the sect. It's not something ordinary, after all."

"Not something you would be proud of either. He might not be keen to let a skeleton out of the cupboard."

Guillaume sighed. "You're right, it's probably a dead end." He looked at Sylvie in the eyes. "Look at me, Sylvie. What do you see in my eyes?"

"You have an idea. Am I supposed to guess what it is?"

"No, you'll soon find out. Do you see anything special?"

"Actually, I'm a bit freaked out Guillaume. What do you want from me?"

"Please Sylvie, just go to the typewriter."

Sylvie did as she was told. She sat down, looked at the keyboard and turned to Guillaume. "Now what?"

"I was hoping it would light up and you would see my life, like it did for Hervé and Sophie after I had seen the sorrow of having lost a loved one in their eyes. That's the trigger—"

"What for, so I could change something?" She turned back to the machine, but nothing happened. "Maybe it can't be used to alter its owner's life."

"You're probably right. Pity. I wonder if there's a way to unlock it so you can use it to change any life."

"You have to be careful, remember the inscription, 'Corrector beware'."

"So far, nothing catastrophic has happened. It actually turned in my favour. If it had been any other lawyer, he would have proceeded with the case."

"You don't know what happened to Sophie though. We're all connected and a change in one life, even for the better, can have unpredictable impacts on someone else's life."

Guillaume found Sylvie's behaviour odd, it wasn't like her to be cautious. She was always enthusiastic to try new things. Could she be hiding something from him that the typewriter could uncover? It was unlikely, she was very open with him; she trusted him enough that she had come out to him, but no one else from Gevrey, not even her school friends. But changing the past was a tricky business, and not something that anyone could have imagined; it was no wonder that she was rattled.

If I could change the past and stop Bénédicte from going to Laos, she would still be alive, but what would my life be like? I would have grown up with a normal family for a start. When Bénédicte died, Mum and Dad died inside, the only thing that kept Dad going was his winery, but outside the cellar and vineyard, there was nothing. Would I have found my vocation or would I have ended up being handed down the winery? And Bénédicte and Pathana, they could have found work teaching here, but would they have been happy? They wanted to make a difference by helping Laotian children and it wouldn't have been the same here. Sylvie is right, our lives are intertwined, you make a small change here and countless others are affected, it's the butterfly effect.

"Where are you going?" Sylvie asked when she saw Guillaume packing a suitcase two days later.

"Taking the TGV to Nantes tomorrow morning, and then driving to Chantenay-Sur-Loire. I have a feeling I may learn something interesting if I find Monsieur Vattier or his relatives. He is the only link I have to the typewriter. I had nothing planned this week-end anyway, it'll be good to get away."

Sylvie didn't hesitate. "Can I come with you? I've never been to Nantes. I wouldn't mind checking out the music scene while I'm there, and eating some *galettes* of course."

"Sure, why not? If there's room in the TGV of course. Otherwise we can catch up over there."

Sylvie opened the SNCF application on her smart phone. "Which one are you catching?"

"The 8:14."

"Great, it's not full yet." She made the booking and said, "That's a big suitcase for just two days."

"I'm taking the typewriter with me so that I can show it to Monsieur Vattier."

Guillaume refrained from adding that it would be safer with him. He hadn't shared with her his conclusion that the burglar had been after the typewriter; he didn't want to alarm her. He found her decision to come with him very hasty; she seemed more reticent two days and now she was raring to go. He didn't try to understand, he was happy to have her company.

The listening device Aaron had placed worked perfectly. The apartment he was renting was putting a dent in his savings, but the confirmation he had that the typewriter could change the past made it a worthwhile investment. Guillaume had changed two person's lives and saved two other lives. They were small changes, but there was only one way of finding out if the typewriter could make the sort of changes Aaron had in mind. He was going to follow Guillaume until an opportunity to take the typewriter presented itself. He made a booking on the 8:14 high-speed train to Nantes and looked at his wardrobe. He was going to wear casual clothes, his suit had been seen too many times. He had to careful, his half-cousin was suspicious now.

His mother was the only person who knew what he was doing. His superiors thought he was on vacation on the French Riviera. He hadn't called his mother to give an update because he knew her line was tapped, as were the lines of all the relatives and friends of Mossad's operatives.

A whole department at Mossad was devoted to making sure there were no double agents. But then, who was watching those who were watching him? There was no such thing as fool proof security, they all knew that. The whole organisation had been shook up when they discovered that one of their best agents had been working for the Iranians. Aaron had worked with him and was shocked that the lure of money had been stronger than the love of his country. The whole affair had been hushed up, his wife and children had been forcibly moved to New York. He had disappeared never to be seen again, some say he was executed but Aaron wondered if the rumour had been spread to fill the hearts of the personnel with fear.

He chose a white Lacoste polo shirt, a pair of jeans and sunglasses and shaved his moustache.

"A word of advice, avoid the A11 highway, there's a blockade," the car hire employee at the Nantes railway station said. "The farmers are protesting against the new EU regulations on pork farming. It's typical of Brussels, isn't it? There's an outbreak of swine flu in Poland and then all the other countries have to comply with the new regulations. It's really hard for them. They invested to comply with the groundwater protection directives, but the supermarkets didn't accept that the costs should be passed on—"

"Thanks very much for your advice, but we're just going to be driving on the small roads," Guillaume said.

"Ah yes, the charms of driving in the countryside, going at your own pace, discovering wonderful little villages—"

"Yes, Yes. Can I please have the keys."

"Here you are, have a wonderful time, Monsieur and your lovely companion, despite the rain."

"That's normal for Brittany, isn't it?" Sylvie asked.

"For your information, the Loire-Atlantique department is not part of Brittany. The traditionalists will tell you that it was part of the historical region of Brittany, but—"

The two friends left before he finished and went to look for their car.

"What a chatterbox!" Sylvie said.

"His girlfriend dumped him last night; he's just trying to distract himself by talking."

"Is that another of your visions? It must be tiring to see everyone's problems." She looked at the cars in the parking.

"Have you noticed all the stickers with the Brittany flag and 44=BZH?"

"44 is the number of the Loire-Atlantique department and BZH is the abbreviation of Breizh, the Breton name of Brittany. What do they expect, it's a lost cause. Ah, here's our car."

Guillaume entered the address of Marcel Vattier in the car's GPS; it was a short drive from the station to the village which had become a suburb of Nantes.

He knocked on the door of the little house which had all its shutters closed.

"It doesn't look like anyone's in," Guillaume said.

"Let's try the house next door."

As they approached, they heard the voice of Jean-Pierre Pernaut, the presenter of the lunchtime news, coming from a television inside. A plaque on the wall informed that this house had been the holiday home of Jules Verne's parents. Guillaume rang the doorbell several times before the door was opened by an old lady.

"Sorry to bother you, Madame, I'm looking for Monsieur Vattier. I believe he lives next door. Is he away at the moment?"

"Monsieur Vattier? He used to live next door. Not that I ever saw him. He kept to himself and never went out. His younger sister Antoinette used to come and look after him, she drove every day from Rezé until she broke her leg. Then she had to find a place for him in a nursing home. I saw them take him away three months ago. He wasn't happy, I can tell you that. He insulted everyone for disposing of him in a rubbish dump."

"Do you know which nursing home?"

"It's in Nantes, but I don't remember the name. Something to do with trees, *Les bouleaux* or *Les peupliers*, I think."

"What about his sister? She would know."

"Antoinette? She passed away last week. I have a friend in Rezé who went to the funeral. A really sweet lady she was, nothing like her brother. That's all I can tell you I'm afraid. Now if you don't mind, I don't want to miss today's episode of the young and the restless. I want to know what Victor is going to do when he finds out what Adam did."

"Monsieur Vattier doesn't sound like an easy man to deal with," Sylvie said as they walked back to the car.

"It's worth a try anyway. Can you look up the nursing homes in Nantes?"

"I already did. It must be *Les Peupliers*. 45 Avenue du Beneuch, I'll enter it in the GPS."

The nursing home was in a nineteenth century bourgeois residence reached by a driveway lined with poplar trees after which the home was named. As they entered, Guillaume looked at the furniture and the paintings.

"I wonder who's paying for it now that Antoinette has passed away. It must be expensive if the rest of the home is like that."

"*Bonjour* Madame, I would like to see Monsieur Vattier," Guillaume said to the receptionist.

"Monsieur Vattier? You're his first visitors since he arrived, are you relatives?"

"Yes, you could say we're distant relatives."

"I'll let him know he's got visitors."

When she came back, Guillaume could tell what Marcel's reaction had been by the look on the receptionist's face.

"I'm sorry, he flatly refuses to see anyone."

"Can you let him know that I have an object that belonged to his great great uncle. It's a typewriter and I would like to show it to him."

"I don't think that he'll be interested, but I can try."

Five minutes later, the receptionist introduced Guillaume and Sylvie to Marcel Vattier, whose eyes went straight to the typewriter, ignoring his visitors.

"It certainly looks like my great great uncle's typewriter," Marcel said. "But I thought it had been destroyed. It can't be a copy, very few people had the privilege of seeing it. Where did you get it?"

"I inherited it from my grandfather," Guillaume said, "but he had locked it away in a trunk and he had never spoken to anyone about it. The keyboard layout pointed me in the direction of your great great uncle. I had it carbon dated, that's how I know it was made in his lifetime. But can you tell us about how it was made?"

The old man lowered his eyebrows and looked at Guillaume and Sylvie with a probing gaze, as if he was assessing them.

"I have to ask you a question first, have you used it?"

The old man's intense look told Guillaume that he would see right through him if he lied. "Yes, I have. It seems that it has some very unusual and powerful properties, although it took me some time to believe that they were real."

"You must be very careful young man. You have no idea what damage it's already caused."

"I presume that's the reason for the inscription."

"Corrector Beware. Yes, Émile put that after an unfortunate incident, and he also put some safeguards. Now close the door and I'll turn on my radio. The walls are very thin here."

Guillaume did what Marcel asked him to do. The old man drank a glass of water before starting his account.

"I won't pretend I know everything. This story has been recorded in Émile's diaries, but if that was the only source, you could be forgiven for thinking it was a work of fiction. After all, Émile was a friend of the great Jules Verne. I sometimes wonder if he gave Jules a few ideas for his books. No, this story has also been passed down from generation to generation, but only from father to son."

"So your sister knew nothing about it?"

"No, women can't be trusted with these things."

Sylvie gave him a dark look, but he continued.

"I'm the last male descendant of the Vattier family and I didn't mind that after my death no living soul would have known about the typewriter; it has brought nothing but trouble."

He paused to look at Guillaume. "You can make up your own mind after hearing this story, but if you want my advice, destroy it before it's too late." He cleared his throat before continuing. "My great great uncle was the eldest of three boys. His father was a teacher and collected books. They nourished Émile's insatiable hunger for knowledge. He loved to pull apart contraptions to see what was inside and how they worked. Clocks and watches for example. You had to keep them away from him if you didn't want them pulled apart. Although after a while he did get better at putting them back together. He drew imaginary machines and took inspiration from Leonardo Da Vinci. He was also interested in esoteric matters, the magic powers of druids for example. When he learnt that the Celts believed that the gods lived in crystal palaces, he started collecting crystals. He used them for all sorts of experiments. It was around that time that he claimed he had a vision where Jesus Christ was brought to earth by a spaceship which the wise men mistook for a star. He was an alien being with great powers who came from a planet where war and death didn't exist, and he tried to instil his wisdom to his disciples. His spaceship came to take him back on the day of the ascension. Émile founded the holy church of Suthci after his vision. The first members were his brothers Léon and Joseph. He was very persuasive and spoke with such conviction that after three months the church had two hundred members. They bought an old farm in Chantenay-sur-Loire and congregated there. It was at this time that he made the typewriter."

A talk show was being broadcast but Guillaume and Sylvie didn't notice it, Marcel had all their attention. They moved closer to him as his voice was starting to weaken.

"The first time he used it was to prevent an accident that had cost his cousin Gauthier the usage of his legs. It worked but Gauthier boasted about it and Émile had to hide it after a church member tried to take it to stop Jesus from being crucified. Can you imagine the consequences?"

Guillaume found it difficult, without Christ's death and resurrection the Christian religion that had shaped western civilisation would not have existed.

"The next year, Joseph was shot dead and when Émile attended the trial, he recognised the culprit. He was a man he had saved six months ago. Émile realised that changing the past was dangerous. He couldn't predict the behaviour of those who were affected by the changes he made. If he hadn't saved that man, his brother would still be alive.

That's when he put limits on what stories could be changed and inscribed the warning message. But he knew that even with that safeguard, unintended consequences could result. In a way, he was right; word got round that there were peculiar things happening at the farm and the villagers got together to get rid of the Satanists they thought were putting curses on their cattle. You see, there was an outbreak of foot and mouth disease that year. The leader of the mob was a cousin of Émile, would you believe. He had asked Émile to make him a rich man and he had refused. The farm was burnt to ashes and the church members that were gathered for the Ash Thursday celebrations all perished. Except for Émile and Léon."

"As you can imagine, that was the end of the church of Suthci. Everyone thought that Émile and Léon had died in the fire, but in fact Émile joined the missionaries in Indochina and Léon went to Quebec to work as a lumberjack. Like my grandfather, I believed that the typewriter had been destroyed in the fire, until today. Émile probably wanted no one to know that it still existed and he must have taken it with him to Indochina."

"I don't remember my grandfather going there, it must have been moved to another country after Émile died. You mentioned his diaries, where are they?" Guillaume asked.

"I've lost them, but why does it matter now? You have the typewriter, what more do you want? Now if you'll excuse me, this talking has exhausted me." Marcel got up to show Guillaume and Sylvie out of his room.

"He was lying." Guillaume said as they got in the car. "He still has the diaries and they must contain something he doesn't want us to find out."

"Then there's no way we can get them," Sylvie said.

"Unless they're still in his house."

"What are you going to do, break in and search the house?"

Guillaume hesitated before saying "No, I'm not cut out to be a burglar. But I have another idea."

Sylvie looked worried. "What's that?"

"Marcel said something about the druids. If Émile found their secrets, why couldn't we?"

"Where are you going to look?"

"We could start by doing some research at the Nantes history museum. I've heard they have a collection of old manuscripts." Guillaume saw the frown on Sylvie's face. "You don't have to come if you have better things to do,"

Sylvie shook her head. "No, I'm coming with you, you need all the help you can get. Let's go."

Guillaume drove to the castle of the dukes of Brittany which housed the Nantes history museum. It was located in Nantes, on the right bank of the Loire River which formerly fed its ditches.

Sylvie read the information on the museum's web site. "The dukes of Brittany lived there between the thirteenth and sixteenth century. Nantes was the centre of the historical province of Brittany until the separation of the Loire-Atlantique department in 1941. The separation isn't old history, no wonder people here are still attached to Brittany."

Guillaume parked the car and they walked to the drawbridge; they found their way to the museum and Guillaume asked the first guide they saw if there were any manuscripts on the druids.

"They left no written accounts of themselves," The guide said. "But there are some descriptions left by the Greeks and the Romans, Julius Caesar in particular, and the legends that were transmitted orally and transcribed by medieval authors. We get these questions all the time. Some people who read the adventures of Astérix and see Julius Caesar in them, assume that the other characters really existed. The rooms on the life of the Gauls are very popular."

"Is it possible to see the manuscripts?" Guillaume asked.

"I'm sorry, but they're in a section that is closed to the general public. You have to make a request for special access."

Guillaume handed his card. "I'm an obstetrician, and this is my assistant. I'm doing some research on obstetrical practices throughout history. The ancients had an intimate knowledge of herbs and there were some that helped women in labour."

"That's interesting. I'm three months pregnant, but it doesn't show yet. I want a natural birth, no epidural or anything like that. I know a good herbalist and he's recommended some herbal teas. I can give you his address."

Guillaume put on his best smile, the one that women couldn't resist. "That's very kind of you, but I prefer to have a look at some of those manuscripts."

"I'll let you in, but promise not to tell anyone. There's a reservation in one hour, so you'll have to be quick. It's a professor from the university." She opened the door of the room. She walked over to a table where pages of a manuscript were laid out underneath a glass panel. "This one is about Fredong, he was renowned for his ability to cure diseases. But you had to be careful not to upset him, he could turn you into a wolf, or if he was in a bad mood into a newt."

Guillaume tried to read it, but he couldn't understand a word. "Is it written in Breton?"

"Yes, they all are. French wasn't spoken in Brittany until the 15th century."

"Yes, I hadn't thought of that."

"There are translations of some of the manuscripts in the library, if you want."

"Thank you very much, you've been very helpful," Guillaume said as they left.

There was a *crêperie* near the museum; the two friends sat at a table and ordered some *galettes*.

"Marcel said that Émile had experimented with crystals and Gilles said that there were crystals inside the typewriter," Guillaume said. "It must be where its power comes from. Émile must have found some nearby. Let's do a bit of digging around."

Sylvie put her glass of cider down. "How's that going to help?"

"I don't know yet, but we've got another day here, let's put it to good use."

"But where are we going to dig?"

"There's Wi-Fi here, look up crystals in Loire-Atlantique."

"Slow down Guillaume, it's been a long day and I'm famished! I'm going to eat my *galette* first."

"Can I borrow your phone then?"

"Sure, go for it."

Guillaume didn't have a smart phone, but he was starting to see their usefulness.

"There are a few places around Nantes. This one looks interesting, it's the hill of Fredong. He's the druid the museum guide mentioned. Legend has it that he was buried there, but no one has ever found his remains."

"I don't fancy your chances of finding anything, but I'll come with you."

"Hey, there's a flea market tomorrow morning, we can check it out before we go. Let's get up at six so we have enough time."

Sylvie yawned. "Oh great, I was looking forward to sleeping in."

"It looks like everyone's emptied their attic and dumped the contents here," Guillaume said when he saw what was on sale at the flea market. "But you never know, there might be some treasures.' He pointed to the left. "Like that mantel clock over there." Guillaume rushed to a table where the seller, a middle-aged man with a thick moustache and a bulbous nose, was arranging his items.

"*Bonjour* Monsieur, how much are you asking for that clock?" Guillaume asked.

"Six hundred euros. As you can see, it's in good condition. It was made during the first empire, I would say around 1810."

Guillaume took the clock in his hands and examined it from every angle. The base was made of red marble and the clock face was enamelled.

"I don't think so, Monsieur, it's a beautiful piece, but it's not empire. It was made in the late nineteenth century. It's not worth more than three hundred euros."

The man's nostrils flared and his face reddened. "You think you know it all don't you? You Parisians are all the same, you come here like you own the place and everyone has to bow to you. My father fought in the war you know."

Guillaume put the clock down and made his way to another section of the market with Sylvie. "That clock was stolen anyway."

"Wow, you'd make a good cop if you ever wanted a change."

"No thanks. In fact, I wish I could turn off my visions when I don't need them. Let's go now, I don't think I'll find anything here."

Sylvie pointed to a table near the exit. "Hey look at those beautiful crystals."

"Where did you find these?" Guillaume asked the old man.

"There are some spots here and there," the man replied dismissively.

"What about the hill of Fredong?"

"No, there's nothing there. Don't waste your time. You'd be better off going to the Gavre forest. See this one, I found it there."

"Thanks very much Monsieur." He walked away and turned to Sylvie. "Well that confirms what I thought, the hill of Fredong is the place to go."

"What do you mean? He said there was nothing there."

"That's because he didn't want strangers digging in his territory. It's like mushrooms. Have you ever heard a mushroom gatherer reveal his best spots?"

"I'm not into mushrooms, I wouldn't know a cep from a death cap."

"Louis was an expert, just thinking about his mushroom omelettes whets my appetite."

The hill of Fredong was a short drive from Nantes. Guillaume parked the car on the side of the road. A rusty gate barred access to a track leading to the hill, hidden by a patch of fog. A rusty chain, a padlock and a sign in Breton were the silent guardians of the druid's resting place. The two friends climbed over the gate and started walking on the track. On either side laid golden fields with fresh bales of hay, caressed by the morning sun piercing through the clouds. Oak trees were standing at the end of the track like sentinels. There wasn't a sound and the two friends didn't say anything, each of them deep in their thoughts.

As soon as they entered the forest, the temperature dropped sharply and they shivered. The track continued, but narrowed to a trail that only walkers could use. Trees had grown on top of the boulders, their roots spreading down to the ground. The slope of the trail increased and the pace of the two walkers slowed down. Sylvie asked Guillaume if they could stop to rest.

While she got a muesli bar out of her bag, he went to the side, attracted by a sparkling rock. He bent down to look at the small crystals that were covering the surface of a boulder. As he looked up he saw another one a few metres above. He continued climbing, following a glittering trail until he arrived at the entrance of a cave. He found a way inside by squeezing himself between two roots. He searched inside his backpack for a torch. The light revealed that the sides and the roof of the cave were covered with crystals of a multitude of colours: red, orange, yellow, green, pink, blue and violet. It was like being inside a giant geode. His contemplation was interrupted by a cavernous voice.

"Here you are."

Guillaume turned around and saw a man in a white robe. He had long white hair and a beard, and wore a gold necklace with a cross-shaped crystal.

"Who are you?"

"I am the guardian of destiny, Guillaume. Each being has a destiny that has been determined before his life, according to what he has done in his previous life. It determines where he will be born and what he will be given to fulfil it. The order of the cosmos is maintained by this allocation of destinies." The old man raised his voice and looked at Guillaume in the eyes. "But there are evil forces at work; they are trying to get more than their ordained portion of glory, power and wealth. If they succeed, the cosmic order will be broken and the fabric of the universe will collapse."

Guillaume looked at him confused.

"You wonder how this concerns you," the old man continued. "Your destiny is to stop them. If you try to escape it, you will find out that your attempts are futile. You will realise that you don't have a choice when your efforts will eventually lead you back to your destiny." His voice softened. "Open your mind and your heart Guillaume and stay alert. Use the talents you have been given. You will discover them as you continue your journey. Take this with you, it will help you." He gave Guillaume a cross-shaped purple crystal similar to the one he wore.

"One last thing I must tell you before you go. Each life is a thread waiting to be woven into the tapestry of lives gone by. Each thread has a different length and a different colour, according to the destiny of the person, and a different material. A king's thread will be made of silk, a pauper's thread will be made of hessian. But you will find that there is a thread that is not where you think it is. This thread is still waiting and you will find it as you fulfil your destiny." The old man pointed outside. "You know what you have to do, now go!"

Outside the cave, Guillaume pinched himself. If this was a dream, he would wake up lying on the forest floor next to Sylvie. But he didn't. If it wasn't for the crystal in his hand, he would have thought that it was another vision. He had to go back and tell Sylvie what he had seen. He followed the glittering trail back to where he had left her.

He caught his breath and said, "Here I am. I hope you weren't worried that I had gone for so long."

"What are you talking about? I haven't finished my muesli bar yet." She looked at him. "You look awful, what's wrong?"

No sooner had he finished describing what he had seen and heard than she was on her feet, begging him to take her to the magical cave.

"I can't see the trail of crystals anymore, but I remember it was that way, I recognise that boulder."

They arrived at the place that Guillaume recalled; there was a cave, but the entrance was completely obstructed by roots from the trees overhead and thick bushes.

"Are you sure it's here? There's no way you could have got through," Sylvie said.

Guillaume looked confused. "Maybe it's further than I thought, let's keep going. I'll use my Opinel to make cuts in the tree trunks so we don't get lost."

After a fruitless search for another cave, they made their way back and Guillaume used his wood handled pocket knife to cut through the bushes. He shone his torch through the hole he had made, but the cave was barren and empty. There were no crystals and no druid.

Sylvie looked at her friend quizzically.

"Why are you looking at me like that?" Guillaume said.

"What's happening to you? You're starting to confuse your visions with reality."

"What about this crystal he gave me? It's not a figment of my imagination."

She took it in her hand and held it up to the light that was filtering through the trees. She turned around and she looked at the cave entrance through the crystal.

"Guillaume, look. I can see an inscription on the rock surface just above the entrance."

Guillaume took the crystal and tried to decipher what he saw.

"I can see the symbol that's on the typewriter and then some markings. They look quite primitive. Vertical lines with horizontal and diagonal strokes on the right, the left or crossing through. They could be letters, but from what alphabet?"

"Sorry I doubted you. Write it down, we can work out what it means later," Sylvie took a notepad out of her backpack and gave it to Guillaume. She always carried it with her to draw or write what her inspiration whispered to her.

In the high speed train to Paris, Sylvie said to Guillaume, "I've been thinking about what you saw in the cave. There are some common themes with the typewriter; not just the symbol, but also the crystals and destiny."

"What do you mean?",

"You've used the typewriter to change the destinies of four people; probably more because their lives were connected with others. So if someone evil used the typewriter to change lots of destinies, it would destroy the cosmic order, as the druid said."

"Do you think he was a druid?"

"According to your description, he sure looked like one— or at least what we imagine druids to look like."

"But he said something about destiny being determined by previous lives. It sounds like karma to me; it's a Buddhist concept, it has nothing to do with druids. Anyway, I don't believe in a pre-determined destiny. We have our free will and we make our own destiny. We're not actors in a play that follow a script that someone's written for us."

"Yes, but what you do with your life is determined by where you're born and by the people around you; they can stop you from doing what you want. I mean, do you think you could've studied to be a doctor if you were born in a slum in Bangladesh?"

"It's less likely but not impossible."

"Life's just a big lottery. Some people have all the luck, the rest have all the crap."

"Luck isn't everything. There are some who start off on the rubbish dump and get out of it. There are turning points in your life where you stop letting things happen to you and start taking action."

Sylvie was too tired to argue, she changed the subject. "Have you figured out how you're going to stop evil forces from destroying the cosmic order?"

"I wish I had, then I could get on with my life. But anyway it doesn't matter, my old chap Getafix said that I couldn't escape from it, so it will get done regardless."

Sylvie wondered about her destiny; had the abuse been pre-ordained? It was finished now, but she lived with the nightmares, the shame and the guilt. Was it a punishment for who she was, or what she had done in a previous life? If the typewriter could change her life, she would stop that man coming into it. The problem wouldn't be resolved though, he would make another girl suffer. But would the typewriter let her make her torturer die? She didn't deserve her life to be fixed anyway, she just had to move on and maybe that was a better thing.

Guillaume was on a quest to fix his past, but he had been warned, the typewriter could do more harm than good. He didn't know what consequence stopping Bénédicte from losing her life in Laos would have. On the other hand, if she told him, would it make a difference? Faced with a choice between his sister and his friend, he would probably choose the former and she didn't blame him for that.

Sylvie thought about death. Like everyone, she lived with a fear of dying. She was convinced that even church goers who were promised eternal life were as scared as she was. 'Eternity is very long, especially near the end', Woody Allen had said, she loved his sense of humour.

She had read accounts of Near Death Experiences, where the person sees her life flashing before her eyes and a tunnel with a light at the end. Many of those who had experienced one said that they didn't want to come back to earth, but were told that their time wasn't up yet. Bénédicte was in a better place now, but Guillaume hadn't asked her whether she wanted to come back. He didn't believe in life after death. He thought Near Death Experiences were hallucinations provoked by a chemical imbalance in the brain. But those who had one were never the same after, regardless of whether they were Christian, Buddhist or atheist. They said that they met a being who embodied pure love and compassion and asked them what they did with their lives. She imagined her response.

What do you expect from me? After what I went through, I did what I could. I was on my own to deal with the pain, you didn't send a guardian angel to protect me, was it because I wasn't good enough?

She looked at Guillaume; he had fallen asleep. He had been seeing a lot of things lately, how much longer could she keep the truth from him?

Chapter Six

28th July, Paris.

Aaron removed his ear-piece and switched on the automatic recording that was triggered whenever a sound was detected in Guillaume's apartment. He was going to listen to it later, he was impatient to read Émile's diaries. They had been well hidden under a floorboard, easy to find when you had the skills, the tools and the determination of one of Mossad's top agents.

He had been given some of the most sensitive missions in the history of the secret service. No outsider knew that he had averted world war three when he had executed a Russian nuclear scientist who had defected and was en route to Iran. His suitcase contained the plans to make a nuclear missile that would be undetected by Israel's radars.

That was the problem with being a secret agent, you had no recognition. You just had to get on with the job of saving your country, knowing that you would remain an anonymous cog in a hidden machine. Zohar Yasik, the head of Mossad, was the only one to get the credit. When he had a meeting with the prime minister, he always asked his team to prepare a summary of the latest successful mission at the last minute. If Aaron succeeded in this private mission, he would make sure that it wouldn't go unnoticed. But his time was limited, Zohar thought that he was on holidays in France and he would be waiting for his return to give him another assignment.

He skimmed through the inventor's first diary, it contained nothing of interest to Aaron: notes and drawings of Da Vinci's inventions that Émile had tried to modernise without success. In the second diary, he had made notes on his research on druids and crystals. The third one looked more promising. It had detailed blueprints of the typewriter and mathematical formulas which he used to calculate the alignment of the crystals. This was followed by the account of his first experiments with the typewriter. Aaron could feel Émile's excitement on the pages. It made them difficult to read. The tone changed when he realised that the man he saved had taken his brother's life. More mathematical formulas followed which he used to determine how to limit his machine's powers.

The fourth volume was thinner but written entirely in code. Aaron spent the next two hours trying to decipher it. Émile had devised his own code and it was very complex, he didn't want to leave anything to chance. *Normal*, Aaron thought, *the stakes were huge*. He was going to have to ask an expert, Theo was the man, no encryption resisted him. As a hacker, he had modified the coordinates of strategic enemy sites that were stored in the US Department of Defence computer network, and reduced the prices of all the flights of a major airline to one dollar. He left the US, leaving no trace behind him, and got a job at Mossad by proving that he could easily penetrate their network. Money didn't motivate him, it was the adrenaline rush that he got from breaking into the most elaborate security systems. Just the thrill of it. It gave him a sense of superior power, that nothing could resist him. He thought he was cleverer than anyone. One day, he was bound to meet his match. While Aaron was thinking about his strategy, a conversation in the building across the road was being recorded.

"The inscription is written in Ogham," Sylvie said.
"In what?" Guillaume asked.

"Og... ham," Sylvie repeated slowly. "It's an ancient Celtic alphabet the druids used. Each letter has a tree, a bird, a colour, a meaning and a divination associated with it. Let's have a look at those letters. The first one is G, associated with ivy and the spiral of revelation. R is the elder and means transformation, death and regeneration. It has one of the strongest reputations for magical protection of all the Ogham letters. Hmm, I like this one. U, the mistletoe, represents healing, spiritual growth and connections with the spirit world. Z is the blackthorn, it is symbolic of outside influences on your life and a journey that must be obeyed. Expect the unexpected, accept changes and move on. It teaches us how to find strength and opportunity in adversity. That sounds very appropriate for us, don't you think?"

"It does," Guillaume said, thinking about how he had found his vocation after Bénédicte had lost her life.

"B for birch, it gives guidance on your path. I is the yew, I don't know that one. It means rebirth. And the last one is D, the oak, signifying magical strength, truth and ability to see the invisible. GRUZBID, what does that mean?" Sylvie typed the letters in the search engine, but did not get a result.

"I'll try keying those letters on the typewriter, you never know."

This had no effect.

"I just remembered, there's a square hole at the back where the crystal could fit."

Guillaume inserted the crystal and typed the seven letters. The keys of the typewriter started glowing, but this time the light was purple. He closed his eyes and started typing. When he finished, Sylvie took the sheets from the typewriter and read the text aloud.

Her name was Ruth. She lived in the United Territories of Israel and Palestine. Today was a very special day, her wedding day with Ashad. She had met him in Tel-

Aviv where they both worked. He was a software engineer at JCN, a multi-national company that was specialised in Predictive Information Technology. It allowed devices to detect the mood and thoughts of its user and adapt its behaviour. If you were hungry, your smartphone could suggest places that made your favourite pizzas. She worked in the restaurant where Ashad was a regular lunch time customer. Three months after they had met, he had asked her to marry him. Ruth thought about her good fortune and smiled. He was kind, hard-working, good looking and loved to write poems for her. What more could she want?

Her sister Rachel finished brushing Ruth's hair. She was ready. The Levi family made their way to their synagogue in Gaza where Ashad and his family had just arrived. Ashad was led under the wedding canopy by the two fathers while Ruth was led by the two mothers. She walked around the groom seven times when she arrived. The rabbi blessed a glass of wine and the couple tasted it. The groom gave the bride a ring and recited the declaration "Behold, you are consecrated to me with this ring according to the Law of Moses and Israel", before placing it on her right index finger. Ashad broke his glass and crushed it with his right foot, and the guests shouted "Mazel Tov!"

The wedding party travelled to Tel-Aviv in a convoy headed by the limousine that was transporting the couple. They arrived at the Khader family's mosque for the second ceremony.

"Welcome all of you to our mosque," the imam said. "God has been called to witness this wedding twice, once as HaShem and the second time as Allah. We know He is happy to do that. After all, He is eternal and omnipresent, He doesn't have the time management issues that his creatures have, or at least the human ones."

Ruth's mother offered her to Ashad and said, "I give you my daughter in accordance to the Islamic Shari'ah in presence of the witnesses here with the dowry agreed upon. And Allah is our best witness."

Ashad said, "I accept marrying your daughter in accordance to the Islamic Shari'ah in presence of the witnesses here with the dowry agreed upon. And Allah is our best witness."

The imam said, "There is none worthy of worship except Allah and Muhammad is His servant and messenger." He went on to declare the Muslim confession of faith, recited three verses from the Koran and finished with a prayer: "May Allah shower his blessings upon you and may He make your union blessed. May Allah grant you righteous children that will be a comfort to your eyes and allow the love between you to increase over the years, and may He bring you both closer to Him. Amen."

A sumptuous banquet followed the ceremony, with much singing, dancing and ululating. The krenzl, in which Ruth's mother was crowned with a wreath of flowers as her daughters danced around her, was followed by a dabke, in which the guests linked hands to dance in a line, and a sword fight dance. What a beautiful day, Ruth thought, the future is looking bright. We live in a beautiful country that is the envy of the rest of the world, with our high standard of living and low crime rate. She looked at her sister who looked blissful like her, but for another reason; she was due in three months. Next year we'll start a family and our happiness will be complete.

Sylvie put down the sheets and said, "This is pure fantasy; Jews and Palestinians living united in one paradisiac country and marrying under both their religions."

"I know, but I saw Ruth's life as clearly as I saw Hervé and Sophie's lives."

"It could be a parallel universe then."

"Calm down, we're not in a science-fiction movie."

"It's not just science-fiction, there are scientists who actually believe in them. Their hypothesis is that there are an infinite number of universes, and everything that could possibly have happened in our past but didn't, has occurred in the past of some other universes."

"But think of the infinite number of combinations of events."

"Yeah I know, you and I probably don't exist in some of them."

Guillaume scratched his head. "There is a more plausible explanation. The crystal and the letters from the cave have turned it into a machine to see the future. I don't know what year Ruth lived in, it could even be the next century."

"Wow, we can put the fortune tellers out of business."

"I don't need it to tell me what my future holds, I've already mapped it out."

"How can you be so sure?"

Guillaume weighed his response. "Actually, I'm not as sure as I was before I found this typewriter."

Sylvie looked at the sheets. "Well, at least this time you don't have to do anything."

Aaron had heard enough. This typewriter had revealed the biggest threat to Israel's security he had ever known. If Israel and Palestine were to be united as one country, it would be no less than the destruction of Israel as a Jewish state. Muslims would become the ruling majority. Their high fertility rate and the return of Palestinian refugees would make Jews a minority. They would no longer have a homeland. He must not let this happen. This mission was getting bigger and bigger, he could not afford to fail. The whole nation of Israel depended on him. It was a pity his fellow countrymen didn't know it. The only threat they thought they had was to be hit by a Palestinian missile. It was a rare occurrence since the blockade had tightened. Palestine was like a prison now and Israel controlled what and who came in the territories and what and who got out.

Aaron put together a plan of action, there was no room for improvisation. The first thing to do was to ask Theo to decode Émile's diary. There was no problem getting him to keep it secret. He had an appetite for underage girls that could get him in trouble. Aaron had caught him in the act last year and he had promised to keep the secret, thinking that one day it would come in handy. But he couldn't use Mossad's communication channels to contact him. They were monitored and if Zohar Yasik got wind of the affair, he would claim all the credit. He was going to use Rose Petal's Facebook page. He had created it to play a prank on Theo and it almost worked. He was too clever for that. He hadn't used it since, but Theo would know that Aaron was sending him a message. He found a series of photos of young girls in sexy poses. It was easy, there were plenty of them on the web. He opened them using the application that Theo had developed. It encrypted a file inside a digital photo using the sequence of bits that made up the top right quarter of the photo. When viewed in a browser, it looked like an ordinary photo, there was no way of knowing there was a file inside. To limit the risks of interception, a built-in timer erased the file after twenty-four hours. Aaron scanned the pages of the diary he wanted to send to Theo and embedded each image into a photo. He posted them on Rose Petal's Facebook page and sent Theo a message: 'Hi honey, we're all ready to have a good time with you, but don't tell our parents...'

Soon he would have the instructions to unlock the typewriter. But that was only half of the battle, he still had to find a way to get it. That was the hard part. If it wasn't for that damned concierge, Guillaume would not keep it with him all the time. He didn't deserve to have it. If he managed to unlock it, and that seemed highly unlikely since Aaron was the only one to have the information, it would be to bring back to life one person, whereas Aaron was going to save more than six million. For the saved men and women were going to have children, and the saved children were going to grow up and have children themselves. The six million would become ten. He would be the hero of the Jewish people, maybe even president of Israel. The country needed strong leadership, to impose its will and determine its own fate, without outside interference. He was the man who could give his nation what it needed.

Aaron's mood dropped when a flaw in his plan became apparent. How would the resurrected know about the fate they had been saved from? Would this be another mission for which he would get no credit? He downloaded articles on the Shoah from the web; they were the evidence he needed. He pictured himself making an election speech.

"Fellow countrymen and women, I believe I am the best man to lead our glorious nation. Unlike the other candidates who make vain promises that you all know will be broken, I can reveal to you that my actions have made be worthy of this honour. Of the eighteen million Jews living here, ten would not be alive if I hadn't saved them or their parents from a catastrophe greater than any that our people have experienced. I can understand that this fact seems hard to believe and before you dismiss me as a lunatic, please look at this. I must warn you, what you are about to see is horrific. Please do not watch if you are sensitive. It is not fiction, it may look like the product of a twisted writer, but it is an alternative reality that actually happened. I, Aaron Rosenberg, stopped it from happening. How did I do this? Of course I am not HaShem, He let his people be exterminated without lifting a celestial finger. No, I am a mere mortal, like all of you. But with the skills and wisdom granted to me, I devised a machine that can change the past. How can you be sure this is true? I have kept recordings of the fate that you escaped."

He had plenty of time to make his speech perfect. The fundamentalists would not like the reference to God. Too bad, there weren't that many of them anyway. There was a lot of material on the Shoah that Aaron could use, he had to choose the most shocking. How could they not vote for him after seeing what they had avoided? From now on, he had to be very careful, if the Palestinians or any of their friends knew what he was about to do...

It reminded him that there was one question he hadn't thought about. How to stop the unification of Israel and Palestine? If he wiped the Shoah from history, would it still take place? Getting elected would take care of that, he would make sure it couldn't occur. There was a bigger question though, what to do about the Palestinians? The country would not be big enough for the two populaces, the holy land should be only for the Jews. He would think of a way to put things right once this machine was his.

Aaron felt like a new man. He was going to join the ranks of great men who had shaped the world: Napoleon Bonaparte, Einstein or even Bill Gates. They had overcome the odds to become what they were. Aaron, an insignificant bastard that no one cared about... Until the day he would become the master of the Jews' destiny. Aaron thought about his namesake, the first high priest of the Israelites. He was another man who had been overlooked. Moses was remembered for leading his people out of Egypt, but if it wasn't for his elder brother, they would still be there.

What a depressing thought, if I don't want my name to be forgotten, I must change it. How about Hamoshia, the saviour?

"Master, the energy of the evil man is increasing," Anula said to the Master with a distressed voice. "He has gained much knowledge and it's making him more dangerous than ever."

He hadn't told the Master anything he didn't know. He had seen it too, but it hadn't affected him as much as his disciple; he had been expecting it.

"An evil man is plotting to use the Vidhi-Vikalpaka to stop millions from reaping what they have sowed in their past lives," The Master said to his students. "If he succeeds, the cosmic order will be destroyed. This man is governed by hatred, represented by the snake. It is the most destructive of the three poisons, it can lead to violence and war. It is very powerful and generates a lot of energy. This evil man is part of the plan, and yet he threatens it. I have given the doctor an object that will help him and his companion will assist him. Remember, you must be vigilant and alert at all times. You can experience hatred whenever the world or your fellow students are not the way you want them to be."

"Master, what is the antidote to this poison?" one of the students asked.

"It is loving kindness, developed through meditation which transforms evil energy into love. Keep practicing, focus your attention and send the love you have generated to those that need it."

"Yes Master," the students replied in unison, "thy will be done."

The Master was silent for a moment. "There is much evil in the outside world, but what makes man do evil?"

One disciple replied, "His thirst for power?"

Another added, "His greed?"

The Master nodded. "You are both correct, Man has a triple thirst that makes him do evil. The thirst for power, the thirst for pleasure, also known as greed, and there is also the thirst for existence. The quenching of the triple thirst is personified by Mara, the wicked one, the tempter, the king of the heaven of sensual delight and egotistical pleasures. The Padhana Sutta tells how Buddha defeated him."

The Master waited for the noise of the rustling pages to cease before he started reading aloud.

Buddha said, "Here is this multitude exerting all their strength and power against me alone. My mother and father are not here, nor a brother, nor any other relative. But I have these Ten Perfections, like old retainers long cherished at my board. It therefore behoves me to make the Ten

Perfections my shield and my sword, and to strike a blow with them that shall destroy this strong array."

Mara caused a whirlwind to blow, but in vain; he caused a rain-storm to come in order to drown the Buddha, but not a drop wetted his robes; he caused a shower of rocks to come down, but the rocks changed into bouquets; he caused a shower of weapons—swords, spears, and arrows—to rush against him, but they became celestial flowers; he caused a shower of live coals to come down from the sky, but they, too, fell down harmless. In the same way hot ashes, a shower of sand, and a shower of mud were transmuted into celestial ointments. At last he caused a darkness, but it disappeared before Buddha, as the night vanishes before the sun. Mara shouted: "Siddhartha, arise from the seat. It does not belong to you. It belongs to me." Buddha replied: "Mara, you have not fulfilled the ten perfections. This seat does not belong to you, but to me, who have fulfilled the ten perfections." The earth thundered to bear Buddha witness. Mara's elephant fell upon its knees and all the followers of Mara fled away in all directions.

111

The Master looked at his disciples. "This story teaches us that evil can be defeated but never destroyed. Good and evil are like light and darkness, one can't exist without the other. Maleficent forces are as necessary as beneficent forces to support the law of karma that ensures that every action had a consequence. Weak and ignorant men follow Mara and do malevolent deeds while the others follow the enlightened one. Every man reaps what he sowed, now or in the future."

The evil man will be defeated, he thought, *like Siddhartha defeated Mara*. He pictured himself watching Mara fleeing, he had the face of Aaron. He had spent his life preparing for this moment, he wasn't going to let anything or anyone get in his way. The survival of the universe depended on him.

Night had fallen and millions of lights had switched on in Paris to prove that it was worthy of its reputation of city of light. Guillaume was reading online discussions on the resolution of the Israeli-Palestinian conflict, when his pager buzzed. He called a taxi and switched off the television and the light. He left a note for Sylvie who had fallen asleep, to tell her he had gone to work.

When Guillaume arrived, he saw that this was no ordinary emergency. Madame Morriset's stomach had swollen and her breathing was laboured. He asked her to pass urine, it was dark. He performed an ultrasound which confirmed the diagnostic.

He turned to the Nurse. "The patient is suffering from Ovarian Hyper Stimulation Syndrome; it's a rare side effect from hormonal stimulation. The fluid that rushed to fill the follicles that the eggs were removed from has spread into the stomach, heart, lungs and kidneys."

He was about to ask the nurse to put the patient on a drip and to administer Pethidine for the pain, when he felt his trouser pocket heating up. He put his right hand in his pocket; the heat was coming from the crystal. He put his left hand on Madame Morriset's stomach and he felt the heat moving from the crystal to his patient who started to relax, while the nurse watched in silence. He stayed like this until the heat had finished its journey. Madame Morriset's breathing returned to normal and the swelling abated.

She smiled and said, "What happened, Docteur? I felt warmth spreading in my body and then the pain stopped."

Guillaume didn't reply, he wanted to be sure. He performed another ultrasound and saw that the fluids were now in the bladder, ready to be eliminated. The nurse watched him, trying to understand. No doubt about it, the crystal had healed Madame Morriset from a potentially fatal condition.

"You had Ovarian Hyper Stimulation Syndrome; remember, I mentioned it as one of the risks when you started the hormonal treatment. But you were very lucky, your body healed itself."

"Leave her under observation for the rest of the night, and call me if the symptoms appear again," he said to the nurse.

He went to the staff room to have a rest before going, and saw Claire, the head midwife. She smiled at him and he smiled back. He esteemed her and saw in her eyes that it was mutual. He poured himself a glass of water and sat down. As he looked at her eyes, he saw that she was affected by the loss of a loved one that she had never seen. He asked her, "If you had a chance to change something in your past, what would it be?"

"I don't know, I can't say I've asked myself that question before." Claire replied. "I consider myself lucky. I have a kind husband and three beautiful children who are in good health and who love me. I love my job, it's really what I wanted to do. I never tire of guiding mothers through their pregnancy and sharing with them their joy of giving birth."

She took a sip from her coffee. "But now that you mention it, there is one thing. If I could change something in my past, I would make my natural mother leave me her name and her photo. I would find her and tell her that I've had a great life. My children would know their natural grandmother." She let a tear flow. "She abandoned me because she wanted me to have a good life, and I did. I was adopted when I was three months, and my adoptive parents always kept a place in their heart for her. They were grateful that she gave them the greatest gift of all, to be parents. They knew how hard it must have been for her and for me; it was, and it still is. There's a battle raging inside of me, between a voice that says, 'She did the right thing, you wouldn't live the life you do if she had kept you' and a vicious one that says, 'She dumped you in a rubbish bin because you're good for nothing'. The first is the strongest, most of the time. I only blame her for her act when the second voice wins. I feel hatred for her. I cry, 'Why did you do this to me, you bitch?' But it doesn't last, I feel remorse for having thought that she was a bad woman. She was abandoned herself you see. As soon as he heard she was pregnant, my natural father left her. Her family gave her no support, they pushed her to abandon me. She had no resources, she could count on no one. She was from a modest background. She didn't have any qualifications and the social benefits wouldn't have been enough to raise me. She was courageous to give up her baby, and also selfless. She wanted me to have a better life than the one I would have had with her. I know this from the social worker I saw when I started looking for answers on my identity. It was all in the file, even her name. But I couldn't have it. The social worker who dealt with my mother's case pushed her to abandon me under secrecy."

She paused to listen to the sound of the ward. A baby cried, two nurses shared a joke. Nothing needed her attention.

"France is one of few countries that allow mothers to do this, apparently to reduce the number of mothers throwing babies in rubbish bins or in the rivers. That's what used to happen, can you imagine that?"

Guillaume shook his head and thought of the countries where today this still happened, particularly for baby girls.

Claire continued. "The law was changed two years ago to allow abandoned children to request social services to contact their mother. Mothers can still refuse the contact, but it gives the children hope. As soon as I heard that, I wrote to the department of social services. They replied six months later, saying that they had searched through the central civil registry and found that she deceased a year ago. They still couldn't give me her name though. What were they afraid of, that I would hassle her children, if she had any after me?"

Guillaume shook his head again, in sympathy. "The law doesn't go far enough, it's a basic human right to know where you come from."

"If the law had been changed six months earlier, I would've been able to contact her, but now I don't know if have any half-brothers or sisters, or nephews and nieces. When I look at myself in the mirror, I try to imagine what she looked like, but it's hard. If I had a photo of her, who would it hurt? She will always have a big place in my heart. Of course, it doesn't stop me from loving my adoptive parents. They've always been there for me, knowing that my heart was big enough for them and my natural mother."

Guillaume looked at his colleague with compassion and admiration. She had lived her life without knowing her parents, but had no bitterness. He remembered the mothers in the ward that had abandoned their children. Claire wasn't judgemental, she did her best to comfort those mothers who had made a difficult decision. She took photos of the babies and the mothers if they agreed to leave them in the file that the social workers constituted. She added notes of how the delivery went and left a personal message to wish the child a happy life. She gave something to those children that she had been deprived of.

A lump formed in Guillaume's throat. Claire's loss echoed his own. They were both grieving the intangible, there was no grave they could cry on. All they had were the words they had heard—in his case a voice from a foreign land carried ten thousand kilometres by telephone wires, in her case a bureaucrat following rules that had been made by those who didn't know what it was like to live without their roots.

The typewriter could give him the power to grant her wish; it didn't seem like a major change, but there could be unintended consequences. If she met her natural mother, she might want to spend more time with her. Her natural parents said that they were grateful to her, but would they feel the same way?

In the building across the road from number 5, Rue de Sévigné, Aaron had noticed that Guillaume had forgotten to take the typewriter with him when he left. He waited for the light in the concierge's apartment to go off. If he moved quickly, he could get what he was after. The concierge had changed the access code but he had heard Guillaume give it to the girl last week.

He was dressed in black and moved silently like a cat. He had executed missions much harder than this one, but the stakes had been much smaller. He breathed in deeply to calm his mind. He didn't want the excitement he had felt when picturing himself in his future position to affect his vigilance. He climbed the stairs slowly and put his hand on his Beretta 9 mm instinctively when he heard the sound of gunshots coming from a television on the second floor. On the third floor, a group of friends laughed at what must have been a dirty joke. Only that sort of joke could provoke such loud laughter.

He opened Guillaume's apartment's door slowly. The darkness was complete, he switched on the flashlight on his headband to find his way. He opened the lounge room door.

He had seen Guillaume leaving the typewriter on the secretaire. It was there, waiting to be returned to the man who would make the best use of it. He was a metre away from it when he instinctively ducked to avoid a large object aimed at him. It crashed on the wall and pieces of metal and shards of glass rained on him. He straightened himself and turned around. His flashlight revealed the girl holding a bass guitar like a club. He moved towards the secretaire and ducked again to avoid being knocked out. The guitar scratched his head and smashed his torch. He couldn't see the girl anymore but he could hear her breathing. He pulled out his gun and fired three shots before receiving the guitar on his arm. He stopped searching for his gun on the floor when a bottle exploded next to him. He got up, ran out of the apartment and down the four flights of stairs, and collided with a group of rugby supporters who had been celebrating France's victory over New Zealand.

"Watch out you jerk!" yelled Didier whom Aaron had pushed over.

"Don't worry bro, I'll teach this moron a lesson," his brother Arnaud said. His hundred kilos and two metres made him a redoubtable front-row forward player at the Aulnay-sous-Bois rugby club. He grabbed Aaron by the arms, head butted him and threw him into an excavation bin. The supporters continued their way after this impromptu amusement.

Aaron stood up and brushed the dust off his clothes before turning into a side street. He didn't want the girl to see that he was living across the road. He had been in difficult situations in his twenty years at Mossad, but it was difficult for him to accept being beaten by a girl and a drunken rugby player. His only consolation is that none of his colleagues would find out. Maybe that was the problem. He was trying to conduct a mission on his own terms. He had to be in the same mindset as if he was on an official mission. This would require a change in strategy. Guillaume and the girl would be taking more precautions now. He couldn't afford to fail, ten million people's lives depended on it.

After a few minutes, Aaron went to his apartment, where he cleaned and bandaged his cuts, and took the shards of glass out with a pair of tweezers. He had seen worse, his ego had suffered the most damage.

Other great men had had their setbacks before their hour of glory. Thomas Edison had failed a thousand times before his light bulb worked. How many billions of them are there now? But how many users of his invention knew his name? Aaron was going to make sure his name would not be forgotten centuries later.

He checked his inbox. Theo 'Lothario' had left a message for Rose Petal: 'Thanks for the wonderful night we spent together. I loved the movie but didn't understand the ending.' A photo of the poster of the movie *Evil blood* was attached. Aaron opened it with Theo's application and read his message.

> It was a tough one to crack, but I love challenges. What is this job you're doing on the side? I don't understand what this is about but it sounds interesting. Of course you have my word this will stay between us just like that other business of mine. There are some really cute ones where I am. They can't resist the thrill of going out with a spy.

Aaron skipped the rest, he wasn't interested in his sordid occupation. It could become a security problem if other agencies happened to recruit underage girls. Iran and other Muslim nations weren't likely to do that, but you could never be sure about anything.

The locking and unlocking of the typewriter involved the insertion of a cross-shaped crystal, presumably the one Guillaume had found. But this had to be done four times, and a different sequence of characters needed to be typed each time. If the instructions were not followed, the effects were unpredictable. If Guillaume had changed it into a machine to tell the future rather than change the past, Aaron would find a way to put it the way it should be.

Sylvie switched on the light to assess the damage. She was unscathed, that was the main thing, and the typewriter was intact. As for the lounge-room, it looked like the battle scene it had been: Red wine (was there blood as well?) spilled out on the floor from a smashed bottle of Wild Duck Creek, the astronomical clock smashed to pieces, two bullet holes in the wall and a third in her guitar which was still in one piece. If it hadn't been for her, the typewriter would be in the hands of a dangerous thief. What was he intending to do with it?

When she heard the sound of the key in the door, she grabbed her guitar and prepared to live her last moments. If he had come back with reinforcements, she wouldn't be strong enough to defeat a whole battalion. She put down her guitar when she saw that Guillaume was here and ran to hug him.

"Guillaume, thank God it's you!"

"Sylvie... what... happened?"

She slumped onto the sofa, pressed her palm on her heart and let out a huge breath. "When I woke up, you were gone and it was dark. I was about to switch on the light when I saw a man with a torch walking towards the secretaire. I didn't have any time to think, I grabbed the closest thing and threw it at him. He ducked just in time. I grabbed my guitar to knock him out, but he ducked again. It smashed his torch, which saved me because as I threw my guitar at him, he shot three times. Then I threw a bottle at him and he ran off. Oh Guillaume, I'm sorry about your clock, I know it was your favourite."

Guillaume looked at her with admiration. "Look, I don't know who this man is, but he nearly killed you. You're lucky to be alive, who cares about the clock? You're incredibly brave Sylvie. I bet he didn't expect the typewriter would be so well guarded."

"Do you think he was the same man the concierge saw the other day?"

"That's very likely. But why go to so much trouble? He must want this really badly to kill for it."

"That means he must know about its power. But how did he know that it was here?"

"No one knew about it until Louis passed away, except Marcel, but he thought it had been destroyed. The only other person who's seen it is Gilles, but I trust him." Guillaume paused before exclaiming, "It must be Louis, he must have talked to someone about it. Whoever it was found out that Louis had passed away, and traced it to me."

"Do you think the burglar knew your granddad?"

Guillaume considered this for a moment. "From what you've described, he wouldn't be of his generation."

"Maybe Louis knew his father."

"Or his mother."

"But even if he did get his hands on it, he wouldn't be able to do any more with it than we have."

"Unless he knows something we don't..."

Chapter Seven

3rd September, Gevrey-Saint-André.

While the sun was browning the skin of holiday makers on the coasts and mountains of the hexagon (as the French designated their country), it was also playing an essential role in their happiness. Thanks to its rays, sugars were accumulating in the fruits of the vine. Next month, those sugars would be transformed into alcohol to brighten the soul of men and women.

Christophe looked at his vineyard. The Pinot Noir grapes were getting bigger and their colour was changing from green to a deep purple. He thought of the tartaric acid inside the grapes being transformed to malic acid. It was going to contribute to the colour, balance and taste of the wine and protect it from bacteria. While the ingredient of this year's wine was maturing, the vines were storing nutriments which would feed the buds in spring for next year's fruits.

He watched the clouds moving slowly and changing shape. The weather was one of aspects of the terroir that had made the wines of his estate renowned, along with the soil and the topography, but it could also turn against him. On the other side of the hill, a hail storm had destroyed Thierry Lemaitre's vineyard. Winemaking was a combination of luck and skill. Dark clouds were coming from the east, would he be lucky again the next time the elements struck? Christophe shrugged, he knew that not everything could be controlled. He remembered his father praying Saint Vincent, the patron saint of wine growers. But did he expect him to stop a hail storm, or to divert it to the vineyard of the heathen? If that was the case, why was Christophe's vineyard still intact? He only went to mass for Easter, Christmas and the feast of Saint Vincent because everyone in the village went.

No, it didn't make sense. Men who made their living from the soil were at the mercy of Mother Nature, and she dispensed nourishment and destruction randomly. Didn't the bible say 'Rain falls on the just and the unjust'?

Another transformation had taken place, but Mother Nature had no part in it. Life had returned to an approximation of normality for the two friends and their hidden enemy.

After the failed robbery, Guillaume had left the typewriter in a bank safe. At Sylvie's request, he had replaced the apartment's front door by a steel door with a triple lock and combination code. It made her feel relatively safe but she spent more time at Clémentine's apartment now that they were reconciled. Eolia was never mentioned again, although Clémentine changed channels every time an advertisement with the little fairy was broadcast.

The members of The Wild Ones used their annual leave entitlement to rehearse songs for a new CD in the garage of Mathilde, the rhythm guitarist of the band. The songs that Sylvie had written were a mixture of raw energy and mystical themes. *The runes of fate*, *Fredong's last stand* and *Lost in the corridors of time* impressed the other members of the band.

"On what trip have you been on, Pix?" Céline, the drummer, asked after they finished playing the new songs.

"I've been reading a lot and found loads of inspiration. But we don't have enough to fill the CD. We'll need to do four cover songs. I was thinking of a rock version of Bach's *Toccata and fugue in D minor*. You know, like the one Motley

Crue did. And then..." She paused and the rest of the band looked at her expectantly, "the Led Zeppelin song Kashmir." She sang the first verse, "Oh let the sun beat down upon my face, stars to fill my dreams."

Sylvie waited for her friends' reactions. It was a song that the seventies rock band considered their best musical achievement. Sylvie's band had gained confidence, but this challenge was going to stretch their abilities.

"I would never have thought of it. I mean, I'm no Jimmy Page, but wow, let's give it a go!" Sandrine, the lead guitarist, said.

"We can try, but I don't know how it'll sound without keyboards," Mathilde added.

Aaron's 'French vacation' had officially ended. Before he left the city of light, he had extended his lease on the apartment and had connected his receiver to an encrypted internet server. This allowed him to continue listening to the conversations in Guillaume's home wherever he was. Not that there was much to listen to. The typewriter was out of reach now, but Aaron counted on Guillaume not resisting the urge to bring it back to his apartment to use it again. It was only a matter of time before Aaron would be able to make a move. He was a patient man, you had to be in his job.

He was sent to Moscow to monitor the activities of the Russian Mafia. The government was suspected of using it to sell weapons to their strategic but unofficial allies. In case the weapons were used to attack other G20 nations, Russia would deny any involvement. The mafia got a good commission, the Russian leaders had clean hands, everybody was happy.

Guillaume had pushed the druid's words out of his mind, but a dream reminded him that he couldn't escape his destiny. He saw the druid showing him the universe collapsing because Guillaume had failed to accomplish his destiny. He woke up shaking and drenched in sweat.

As he let the hot water of the shower cleanse him and relax him, he thought about his so-called destiny. He was supposed to stop evil forces from destroying the cosmic order. The only evil force he had encountered was the burglar, and if he was intending to use the typewriter to annihilate the universe, he was more evil than Guillaume thought. He couldn't see what else he could do apart from putting the typewriter in a safe place. If there were other evil forces, he hoped the safe was strong enough to resist them. He dreaded hearing on the news that the branch of the Banque Nationale de Paris where the typewriter was stored had been robbed.

After a strong coffee, his rational mind regained control of his thoughts. There was no such thing as destiny. As a doctor, he couldn't accept that everything was pre-determined, and certainly not by an old man hiding in a cave.

The perspective of another lonely Sunday depressed him. Sylvie was with Clémentine; he missed her company but was happy that she was with someone she loved. He would have preferred working today, it would have made him feel useful. But regulations were strictly enforced since Docteur Renouil had started in his role of administrator. Budgets had to be rigorously respected and when Guillaume had offered to do unpaid work, it had been refused on the grounds that he wouldn't be covered by the hospital's liability cover. Guillaume suspected that Docteur Renouil was doing that to make him feel undesirable, but other doctors were also complaining about the increased bureaucracy. He wasn't going to spend the day moping. The sun was shining, he was going to go for a walk with no set itinerary and see where his random steps would lead him, out of defiance to fate.

He walked down rue de Sévigné, turned right onto rue de Rivoli, turned right again onto Rue Maher and then left onto rue des Rosiers, which was closed to traffic on Sundays. It was the heart of the Pletzl, the Jewish district of Paris, although many of the Jewish shops had been replaced by upmarket fashion shops. After having eaten a five-Euro falafel, you could buy yourself a seven hundred-Euro leather designer bag.

He joined the queue at the Finkelstajn bakery to buy a Polish strudel. While he was enjoying the delicious pastry filled with a mixture of almond meal and sugar, he stopped to read the commemorative plaque at what used to be the Goldenberg restaurant. Twenty years ago, two assailants had thrown a grenade and fired shots with their machine-guns. This anti-Semitic attack had taken the lives of six men, although none of them were Jews. While the investigation had concluded that it was perpetrated by members of the Fatah, there had been contradictory leads pointing to a group of neo-Nazis. The bullet holes in the wall had stayed there, bordered by yellow paint. The Jews' philosophy was to never forget, but it was also a reminder that they were never safe, as the desecration of Jewish graves and explosion of bombs near Jewish schools had attested during the years that had followed.

He stopped at a synagogue and joined a guided tour, curious to see what was inside.

"Welcome to this synagogue, or as we say in Yiddish, Schule," the guide said. He was an old rabbi with white hair and a beard, who reminded Guillaume of the druid. "It is the oldest in Paris and is also known as the Schule of the deported because it was the first place that the survivors of the Shoah came to. They were still wearing their striped uniform, you see." He pointed to a lamp above the entry. "This is the sanctuary lamp, it represents the menorah of the temple of Jerusalem. Of course, in those days the light came from olive oil burning. These days it is electric, but there are batteries inside in case of a power cut. It must never go out, because it symbolises God's eternal presence and the light released from the shards of the receptacles that God used to create light and goodness. Now we wouldn't want light and goodness to disappear would we?" His laugh put his visitors at ease.

Guillaume couldn't understand that Jews could still believe in God after the horrors they went through. How could they explain that He had let it happen? Did they see it as a punishment for not being faithful enough? It was another argument against destiny. If there was such a thing, it would mean that before the six million Jews who perished were born, it was decided that they were going to die in concentration camps. It was an insult to the victims and their families.

"Before we conclude this tour, I will be very happy to answer any of your questions on our faith or our place of worship."

None of the visitors had any questions or if they had any, they kept them to themselves.

"There is a question that is often on our visitors' mind, but most of the time, it remains unspoken, as if there was some sort of taboo," the rabbi said, looking at Guillaume. "How can we still believe in God after the Shoah? It is in fact a very old question, for numerous nations and rulers have been determined to wipe us out. Babylon, the Roman, Greek and Egyptian empires, to name but a few. There is nothing new under the sun. And yet Israel remains, which is more than can be said for our enemies." The rabbi paused and looked at his guests, a mixture of locals and tourists, young and old, men and women.

"We were never, ever promised that our journey wouldn't be marred by terrible misery," the rabbi continued. "There's an exegetical story that says that God showed Israel the entire future of the Jewish people if they were to accept the covenant. All the good and all the bad, He didn't leave anything out. Israel accepted the covenant. Since we say that we were all at Sinai at this moment of revelation, we knew and know what is at stake by being Jews. Our theology repeats constantly that we may not understand why bad things happen, but they are part of a greater plan that is good."

Guillaume thought about the vision he had been given of a country where Jews and Palestinians lived in perfect harmony. Was it part of that greater plan, however improbable it seemed?

As he continued his promenade, he looked at the gay bars and shops that had flourished. Another persecuted minority had chosen this neighbourhood, and the two communities lived alongside each other in perfect indifference. Gays had also suffered at the hands of the Nazis, although this was not acknowledged until the 1980s. Today, his best friend didn't feel safe to reveal herself as she really was to her own family.

What a sad world we live in.

On his way home, Guillaume thought about the typewriter. Since he had it, he had a recurring dream where Bénédicte was still alive and calling him to rescue her. It was the same dream that he had had after her death and he had dismissed it, but now it was haunting him again. He had seen it as a message that he could use the typewriter to stop Bénédicte from losing her life. After that hope had been quashed, he had locked up the typewriter, as his grandfather had done. What lives had Louis been able to change before he did? Had he caused a catastrophe or had someone tried to steal it from him? Had he recorded the answers in his diary? Guillaume had searched for it in the apartment, but he couldn't remember what he had done with it. If it was in the hands of the burglar, he wouldn't be able to do anything with it—it was a small consolation.

It was time to do something with his life that he had been preparing for the past twenty years—writing his application letter for Doctors Without Borders. It was where he should be, it was the right moment. Their latest achievement in the obstetric field was a reduction in maternal deaths of more than sixty per cent in the Bo district of Sierra Leone. They ran a two-hundred bed obstetric and paediatric hospital there, and were planning to build another one in a country that had infant maternal and maternal death rates amongst the highest in the world. It was the perfect place for him.

"France Inter news, the time is seven AM," the radio announcer said. "The RATP has announced the first day of a general strike that will leave only twenty-five per cent of services running today. Commuters are advised to make alternative arrangements. Employees are protesting at the planned changes to their retirement benefits. They can currently retire at fifty if they have twenty-five years of service, and their pension is based on the average salary of their last six months. The changes will progressively bring them in line with the general retirement system. Other special retirement schemes that will need to be reformed include *Électricité de France-Gaz de France*, *Banque de France* and *Opéra de Paris*. The government has estimated that over six billion euros a year will be saved by 2016, final year of the implementation schedule."

Guillaume quickly finished his breakfast. It was going to be chaos to commute today. Taxis would be a first choice for most people who didn't have the luxury of staying at home. If he was quick enough, he could get a bicycle at the *Vélib'* rank in Rue Saint Paul.

He didn't feel any sympathy for train and bus drivers. There was no reason they should be treated differently to the rest of the population. Their job wasn't the only one that was difficult. They had more power because they could bring the city to a standstill. He couldn't imagine himself going on strike. The babies who were ready to come couldn't make alternative arrangements.

Guillaume took the last available bicycle and made his way through the clogged arteries of the city. The timing of the strike was perfect, it guaranteed maximum impact. It was the first day back at work for many and it didn't take long for the holiday cheer to be replaced by the usual surliness that Parisians were renowned for.

As he stopped at a traffic light, he saw a girl dressed in black, with piercings in her nose, her chin and her eyebrows. She wasn't the only one dressed like that in the crowd, but what struck Guillaume was the death wish she had in her eyes. He rode on the footpath and blocked her way. "Valérie, don't!"

"Watch where you're going you moron, you scared the hell out of me!"

"But listen to me Valérie, you—"

"How do you know my name?"

"I have a message for you: there's a transport strike today, you won't be able to jump in front of the train. It's a sign that you shouldn't do this."

"Who told you I was gonna do that and what's it to you anyway?"

"Let me buy you a coffee and I'll explain."

"Who are you, some sort of pervert? I don't need anyone's help to die, I'd rather do it on my own terms. So piss off now."

"I'm a doctor at the Pitié-Salpétrière hospital; I just want to stop you from doing something stupid."

"What has Mum been saying about me? She doesn't care anyway."

"Does she work there?"

"Of course she does; How come you know so much about me and you don't even know that my mum works in your hospital?"

"It's a big place; I don't personally know her, but I'm sure she does care about you, she just doesn't show it."

"She never has any time for me; when she's not working, she's sleeping with all the men she meets."

"Is that why you want to end your life?"

She sat down on a bench and lit a cigarette. "No, it's François; he dumped me to go with that slut Sophie."

"Is he really worth dying for?"

"I really believed him when he said he was going to love me forever."

"But there are plenty of other boys out there." He gave her a tissue and she blew her nose. "What do you do in life Valérie?"

"Not much. I dropped out of school when I realised I was good for nothing."

"Do you have any hobbies, like sport or music?"

"I play the synthesizer."

"Have you heard of The Wild Ones?"

"Yeah, they're awesome. I saw them at the *Fête de la musique*."

"Sylvie, the bass guitar player is my flatmate and best friend. I'll talk to her about you, she said that they were missing a keyboard player for some of their songs. She mentioned a Led Zeppelin song, Kashmir I think it was."

Her eyes lit up. "Really? It's one of my favourites—they used a mellotron on that track, it's the ancestor of the sampling synthesizer."

He gave her his card. "Here's my number, call me if you start feeling blue again, and give me your number; I'll get Sylvie to call you."

She wrote her number on a used métro ticket. "Thanks heaps, Doc. Here's my number."

"What are you going to do now?"

She got up. "Go home and practice of course."

Guillaume watched her turn back. She was out of danger, but for how long? He was going to speak to her mother, and Sylvie could watch her too. He took his bicycle and made his way back on the street; when he arrived at the hospital, he saw that he wasn't the only one that had ridden a bicycle to work.

His first delivery was the wife of the imam of the Paris mosque, Halil Benkabou. He stayed in the waiting room, leaving his mother-in-law with her daughter to provide her with help and support. His wife was going to need more comfort than he thought. It was her fifth delivery, but as soon as the monitoring was switched on, the delivery team knew the outcome. Guillaume searched his pocket for the crystal. *Damn, I've left it in the typewriter, it's too late now!*

"Madame, I'm sorry, but your baby's heart is not beating. Nevertheless, it doesn't change the way the delivery takes place."

The woman looked at Guillaume in disbelief, but not for long. She had a job to do, the midwife was urging her to push.

When the baby came out, his grandmother wailed but his mother seemed indifferent. Blood samples were taken to determine the cause of death. An hour later, Guillaume had the results: chlamydia had caused the death, transmitted by the mother who herself had it from the father, who himself had it from... Guillaume wasn't one to judge but it was the sort of information the extreme-right party, Le Front National, would use to their advantage if they had it.

"*Bonsoir* Monsieur Benkabou," Guillaume shook the hand of the imam. "I'm the obstetrician and I'm sorry for your loss. Unfortunately there was nothing you or I could have done. The baby had a bacterial infection and—"

"Don't worry Docteur," the imam said. "It is the will of Allah."

Guillaume couldn't stop himself from asking, "But why would Allah want this to happen?"

"Allah is great and merciful, He is beyond our comprehension. We are tiny creatures whose minds are not capable of answering such questions. We have to trust Him, only then can we surrender to Him. Islam means submission to Allah, that's what our faith is about. You see Docteur, Allah willed everything that has happened and will happen in the universe and has written it down. What is written on the tablet of Allah cannot be changed."

"But didn't Allah create man with his own will?"

"Docteur, you are a man of science, you seek answers to everything. That is true, Allah knows our choices and lets them happen. In fact, in his great wisdom, he has decreed to pass things which He doesn't love and is not pleased with. His wisdom is in all things, even evil, because it can make men return to Allah. Sometimes man is too comfortable and forgets about Allah. When misfortune strikes him, it reminds him of Allah and the necessity of prayer."

Guillaume had never spoken to an imam before. He was far from the image that the media loved to portray, fiery men who exhorted their followers to join the Jihad. He was humble and confident at the same time. Guillaume continued his questioning. "But why do Muslims pray, if Allah has already decided what is going to happen?"

The imam smiled and said, "Supplication to Allah affects what has been written, but the change in what is already written is itself written and ordained. For example, if you are sick and you pray Allah to be cured, both the prayer and the cure are already written. I prayed to Allah that I would have a healthy baby, but I knew that it would only happen if it was Allah's will. I'm a mere mortal, who am I to question what Allah has decided?"

Guillaume was impressed by his arguments; there was an impeccable logic to the imam's faith even if he didn't have the answers to everything. "Thank you for enlightening me on your faith Monsieur. I think I had a wrong impression, that somehow Muslims were, how can I say…"

"Fatalists, is that what you're trying to say? Many people think that. But as a doctor, you must have heard of Avicenna."

"The Persian physician? Yes, I have, he was remarkable. He was the author of the canon of medicine. It was the pre-eminent medical encyclopaedia during several centuries in Europe."

"He wrote it during the golden age of Islam," the imam added, "while Europe was in the dark ages. Muslim scholars like him preserved the knowledge of Greek and Roman physicians from extinction and added to it. He was the first to recommend the use of forceps in deliveries complicated by foetal distress and to discuss the theory that small organisms were responsible for infectious diseases." He smiled. "He wasn't really a fatalist, was he?"

Guillaume shook his head and the imam said, "If you have any other questions on my faith, you know where to find me. We will meet again, Inch' Allah."

Guillaume went to the staff room and pondered what he had heard.

If Allah has willed everything, then the typewriter was his will. But if I'm supposed to stop evil forces from using it to break the cosmic order, that's Allah's will again. On the other hand, if I was going to resist my destiny, Allah would know about it already. So either way, Allah wins. When I decided to be an obstetrician, it was the obvious choice because I wanted to make a difference and redeem Bénédicte's death. I can't imagine myself doing something else now. But what if I changed my mind and became an architect? Who would stop me? Certainly not Allah, but whatever I decide, He already knows about it—

"Guillaume, are you all right?" Claire asked.

"Um, yes, I'm just thinking about my last patient."

Claire's interruption reminded him that there was something in the imam's eyes that Guillaume had seen, but he hadn't paid attention to it at the time. The imam was in danger and he didn't know it. But in danger of what? Could the typewriter provide the answer? A cancelled appointment gave Guillaume the opportunity to go to the bank to open his safe. The safe room was underground. To reach it, you had to go through five steel doors each with three locks. The walls, ceiling and floor of the room were made of steel that tunnel diggers would find impossible to penetrate. Guillaume guessed that the other safes contained jewellery, gold bars and works of art worth millions of euros. The typewriter's value could not be estimated, but someone was prepared to kill for it. That someone hadn't come back, was it because he knew that the typewriter was here? Guillaume shuddered at the thought that he was being watched.

It was cold in the safe room and Guillaume felt he was locked in. It wasn't just a feeling, he really was. He put the typewriter on a table in the middle of the room. The keys started glowing. Guillaume wondered what the security guard was going to think was happening, but discretion was part of his job. The only thing that mattered was the security of the items stored in the safes. Cameras were forbidden, but the rules said nothing about typewriters.

His name was Halil Benkabou. He was the imam of the Paris mosque and a renowned scholar in the field of Abrahamic religions, well known and respected in the Muslim, Jewish and Christian academia.

"Welcome to the Brotherhood of the Children of Abraham," Halil said in a meeting room where priests, rabbis and imams were gathered. "For those of you that are new, our mission is to promote inter-faith dialogue and to be involved in negotiations for peace wherever there are conflicts between followers of the Abrahamic religions. Peace is possible, we all worship the same god under different names. His will is that we live together in harmony and acknowledge that our common ground is greater than our differences. Take Israel and Palestine for example. Muslims and Jews can live together in one united country and I believe that it is only a matter of time before it happens."

He paused to look at the mixed reactions to his last words. He had a lot of work ahead of him to convince everyone, but he was confident. It was Allah's will and he was a conduit for the accomplishment of His will.

"I want to take this opportunity to speak about the other countries where the brotherhood is operating. Israel of course, but also Russia, where I am planning to go in October. We all know about the Jews and the Orthodox Christians in that country, but the Muslim population in Russia is growing. It has a long history: the Islamic presence dates from the 16th Century when Russia conquered the regions of the middle Volga and brought the Tatars into the Russian state."

Six months later, at Moscow airport, Halil saw a man with a sign 'Welcome to Russia, Halil Benkabou'. The man led him to a black car and opened the door. Inside the car, a man in a black suit greeted him.

"Welcome Mister Benkabou, my name is Sergei. I'm the leader of Solntsevskaya Bratva. It's part of what westerners vulgarly refer to as the Russian mafia. A friend of mine told me you were coming, a Mossad agent. You see, Mister Benkabou, the Israelis are not happy about your work to unite Israel and Palestine, they don't like it one bit. And actually, neither do I, because if you succeeded, it would be very bad for business. So how can I put it? It would be very unfortunate for you if you continued to preach the unification of Israel and Palestine."

"Who are you to dictate my actions? I only take orders from Allah, and it is His will."

"Well it's too bad he's not here to defend you. I'm sorry Mister Benkabou, I did warn you, but if you're not prepared to be reasonable, then I'm going to take you to a place where you will never come back."

Guillaume put the sheets in his pocket and the typewriter back in the safe. There was no time to lose, he had to save the imam from being executed by the Russian mafia. He returned to the hospital and consulted the imam's wife's file to find a contact number.

"Monsieur, it's me, your wife's doctor."

"Ah yes, is anything the matter with her?" replied the imam with an anxious voice.

"No, nothing. But you are in great danger."

"What do you mean? Does this have anything to do with the death of my baby?"

"No, it doesn't. Tell me, are you planning to go to Russia?"

"Yes, next month, why?"

"I know this is going to sound absurd, but I ask you to trust me. The Russian mafia are planning to eliminate you."

"But why would they want to do that? And how do you know this?"

"They deal in arms and will do anything to stop peace in the Middle East. I have this information from a very reliable source."

"But this trip is very important to me, and to the Russian Muslims. There are tensions in their country and the message of peace needs to be heard."

"But you don't understand. If the mafia have decided to eliminate you, they will succeed. If there is one thing in Russia that works, it's the mafia."

"I don't think that *you* understand. I'm doing Allah's will and if I have to die while I'm doing it, it's also part of his will."

Guillaume raised his voice, "Well you know what, I'm also doing Allah's will by calling you. He knew that I was going to call you, it was written on His tablets. He wants to save you. Otherwise why would he have given me this information after we had met?"

The imam paused to ponder Guillaume's question. "Docteur, I'm impressed, although I'm not surprised. I knew you were a man of great intellect. You remembered what I told you, and you used it to try to convince me. I'm inclined to believe you because I can't see why you would make up this extraordinary story. I need to think about it and ask Allah for guidance."

I did what I could, if he wants to die a martyr it's his problem.

The phone rang before Guillaume had time to put it back in his pocket; it was his father.

"Guillaume, I won't need your help for the harvest this year," Christophe said.

"Why not? You know I always take two weeks off to help you."

"I know, but Thierry's vineyard has been completely wiped out by a hail storm, and he's proposed to help me. He prefers to take part in the harvest, it will raise his spirits. He says the cleaning up can wait."

"I can come anyway."

"We've got enough hands, why don't you take a real vacation for a change? You haven't done that since you started your studies. Mum and I noticed you looked tired last time we saw you, it'll do you good."

"I don't know where to go."

"It's an ideal time to go anywhere, the weather's still good and the crowds are gone. Or so they say, we've never gone away in September."

Guillaume remembered his vision of a vineyard destroyed by hail; he wasn't surprised it had come true. He consulted his emails; the annual European Obstetric conference was being held in Nice next week. Perfect, it would allow him to enrich his knowledge and do some networking, which could be useful for his application with Doctors Without Borders. He would also feel less guilty about doing nothing. Gilles was from Nice, and had often told Guillaume that it was a beautiful town that everyone fell in love with.

Guillaume arrived in Nice a day early to visit the flea market in the old town, hoping to find another clock. The first day of the congress was going to be busy. Recent advances in medical procedures and treatments were going to be discussed. There were different opinions on how to prevent complications during pregnancy and delivery and reduce maternal and neonatal mortality. The prediction of hypertensive disorders before the onset of preeclampsia was interesting, but what was the point of predicting a condition when an effective prevention plan did not exist?

Guillaume had made his way from his hotel in the heart of the old town to the Cours Saleya when his phone rang. He looked at the screen, it was an unknown number. His eyes on his phone, he walked into a young woman admiring a brooch, making her drop the slice of Socca she had just bought.

"I'm terribly sorry," he said. "Are you alright?"

"Don't worry, I'm fine," she replied with an English accent.

Guillaume looked at her. She was slim and her silky black hair flowed down her face.

"Are *you* alright?" she asked.

"Um, yes. Here, let me buy another slice of Socca."

"It's all right, you don't have to."

"I insist." Guillaume led her to a stall selling the chickpea pancakes that were a speciality of Nice. "I think I'll have one myself, they look delicious."

"I don't know, I didn't get a chance to taste mine." Her laugh lit up her face.

They both took a bite and Guillaume looked at her brown eyes. They sparkled with joy and vitality, but there was something else that he could sense, without being able to define what it was.

"By the way, my name's Guillaume."

"I'm Lien, nice to meet you Guillaume."

"It's a beautiful name."

"It means Lotus in Vietnamese. I'm very grateful to my mother for giving me this name. The Lotus is a beloved flower used to pay tribute to Buddha because it is associated with celestial beings."

For a fleeting moment, she was overcome with emotion, as if speaking about her mother evoked a sad memory. Lien reminded Guillaume of a flower, graceful and fragile. Did she have someone in her life to protect her? Her delicate fingers did not have a ring.

"Are you here... on vacation, or do you live here?"

"It's a long story."

"I have all the time in the world. If you do too, of course."

"I didn't have any plans, I was just going to wander around the market and the Promenade des Anglais. It's such a beautiful day."

"Let me buy you a drink." Guillaume pulled over a chair at a café table. "What will you have?"

Her voice sounded like that of an angel. "An orange juice would be great."

Guillaume felt dizzy. Her smile made him feel weak at the knees. It was a feeling he had never experienced. Completely irrational.

"I'm from Melbourne, in Australia. I'm here by accident, so to speak. My friend Nathalie was in a car crash two weeks ago. She's lucky to be alive. Her boyfriend took the car after he had too much to drink. The idiot drove into a tree. She was really looking forward to this trip to France with him. She couldn't change the dates or get a refund, because he bought the cheapest tickets with strict conditions. She asked me and her other best friend to take their place. I felt guilty leaving her, but she said, 'You've never been overseas before. Go on enjoy yourself. I'll give you a shopping list and you can bring me back a few goodies'. It was very short notice, but the veterinary hospital where I worked agreed."

"I'm sorry about your friend."

"I called her yesterday, she'll be out of hospital in three days. She'll need some rehabilitation though."

"So how long are you staying here?"

"Until the end of the week. I'm going to explore the little villages in the hinterland. I've heard Tourette-sur-Loup and Saint-Paul-de-Vence are really nice. I'm going to enjoy the beautiful art which is everywhere you look. My friend Amélia went to Italy to see her relatives, but we'll catch up in Paris."

Guillaume brought forward his return date so that he could see her again. "I live in Paris, call me when you get there and I can show you around. I'll be at home on Sunday. I'm only here for a few days to attend a congress."

"What sort of congress?"

"On obstetrics, it's for my work."

This revelation troubled her. Guillaume usually didn't tell women about his specialisation. He had found that they weren't attracted by men who spent their time looking at women's reproductive organs. He breathed in deeply to steady his nerves.

She quickly changed the subject. "And what do your parents do?"

"They have a vineyard in a little village in Burgundy."

Again she was troubled, but Guillaume couldn't understand why.

"Have I said something to upset you?"

She finished her glass and said, "It's been lovely talking to you Guillaume, but I must go."

"But wait..."

She got up and walked away without turning her head. Guillaume froze in his seat. He watched her melting into the crowd and disappearing. She had exited his life as suddenly as she had come in. They were two persons living their lives like parallel lines; they should never have crossed, but they did, if only for an hour. An insignificant portion of their lives, sixty minutes out of the forty million or so that they could expect to live. It was no more than a grain of sand on a beach.

How many women had he met in his life? Hundreds in his job where he cared for them during the most important moments of their lives. Dozens in casual encounters that didn't require after-sales service. But something had happened with Lien that he had no control over. It hit him like the proverbial *coup de foudre*, what the French called lightning strike, the English named love at first sight. Is that what it was? Did he fall in love with a complete stranger? How else could he describe the feeling that had touched every cell in his body? He had felt like he was in heaven and she was an angel.

He tried to dismiss what had happened. She lived twenty thousand kilometres away and he had plans for the future that excluded the very idea of love. There was only room in his life for his vocation.

His heart's voice grew louder. "She is your soul mate, the woman that you will spend the rest of your life with. You share a common destiny, fate has brought you together in this time and place".

No, there is no fate, meeting Lien was a fluke. If her friend's partner hadn't driven after having too much to drink, she wouldn't be in France. If hail hadn't destroyed Thierry Lemaitre's vineyard, I would be helping Dad with the harvest. And anyway, she ran away before I had time to give her my number. I must have scared her—just as well, we had no future together.

Guillaume went for a walk on the promenade des Anglais. Tourists were taking photos of the bay of angels, couples were strolling hand in hand and teenagers on their scooters were slaloming through the crowd. His heart wasn't in it. For the first time in his life, he felt solitude. It had been hiding under the surface and the choices he had made in his life kept it there. It had crept up on him when his guard was down. All he had to do was to bury it again. He had other things to do that were more important to the world. Lives needed to be saved, children needed to grow up with their mothers. Nothing was going to stop him from realising his plan.

He consulted his voice mail in his hotel room; there was a message from the imam. He had cancelled his trip to Moscow after praying for guidance and thanked the doctor for his help. It was disappointing in a way. If he had gone and got killed by the mafia, it would have proven that the typewriter was showing the future. But Guillaume couldn't bring himself to believe that the two arch-enemies Israel and Palestine could be united. On the other hand, who would have believed that one day the Berlin wall would fall?

Gilles had given Guillaume the address of an authentic restaurant, but after the waiter brought his *Salade Niçoise*, he realised that he wasn't in the mood for eating anything. He finished his bottle of rosé de Provence and went to a night club to see if he could finish the night in good company. But he had no appetite for girls either, they all look dull to him.

He returned to his hotel room and fell asleep in front of the television.

He dreamt that he was surfing; as he prepared himself to catch a wave, he saw that he was surrounded by sharks. They caught the wave with him, biting at his surf board. The beach was ten metres away, he wouldn't have time to reach it before being eaten. His life flashed before his eyes as he fell in the water and felt his flesh being ripped out. After the dark of the water, he saw a bright light and a soft voice called him. He turned his head and saw Lien smiling at him and assuring him that he was going to be alright now that he was with her.

Twenty-four hours had passed since he had seen Lien and he had managed to push her out of his mind by taking an interest in the effectiveness of corticosteroids in the reduction of morbidity in multiple pregnancies and other matters. But when he saw her waiting for the lift in the hotel lobby, his heart raced. He breathed deeply and walked towards her, not knowing what to say. Was she going to ignore him?

She spoke first. "Guillaume, what are you doing here?"

"Hi Lien. Don't worry, I haven't been following you. I'm staying here."

"Listen, I'm really sorry about yesterday. You must think I'm a very rude person."

"I was worried I'd said something to upset you."

"Not at all. In fact, it's a long story."

He smiled. "Another one? Great, I love your long stories."

She smiled back. "I'm going to my room to change. Let's meet here in half an hour."

Guillaume was back in the lobby twenty minutes later. He watched the lift door anxiously. He couldn't stop his heart from pounding and his palms from sweating.

What if she changed her mind? What a fool, I'm like a teenager before his first date. Is my memory playing tricks on me again? She looked prettier than yesterday, her voice sounded more angelic and her eyes sparkled more.

After fifteen long minutes, Lien stepped out of the lift with a natural grace and elegance Guillaume had never seen before.

They walked into the first café they saw, *Chez Marcel.* Ten tables, a zinc counter, four men concentrated on their game of *belote*, the card game that was a favourite of the French. The place was frozen in the nineteen-fifties, a time when hope had replaced despair, the nation was rebuilding itself, and jobs were plenty, as were the babies who were going to repopulate the country.

"It had nothing to do with you Guillaume. I was afraid."

"Afraid of what?"

"Of not being able to face the truth."

Guillaume looked at her quizzically.

"Let me explain from the start. I was born in a little village in Southern Vietnam in 1978. I was only three months old when my parents left the country in a boat to escape persecution from the socialist government. In fact they also escaped being massacred by the Kampuchean army. They didn't know it at the time, but they left the night before the whole village was destroyed. They boarded a fishing boat with twenty other people." She paused, tears streaming down her face. "The boat was attacked by Thai pirates. They stole what little valuables the passengers had. They took the women with them, including my mother. My father was helpless. If he had made a move to rescue her, they would have killed him. The men saw that they had no choice but to continue."

"Lien, I'm sorry about your Mum, I had no idea."

"You couldn't know." She wiped her face. "I grew up without a mother, it left a hole in my heart that nothing can fill. My father described her to me. She was kind, beautiful and hard-working. She was an invisible role model for me. I worked hard to be a veterinarian, I wanted her to be proud of me. In her village, she was known as the animal healer. She knew the remedies for all sorts of ailments the animals had. One day, I'll move to the country to look after farm animals like my mother did." She paused. "When the men and children arrived on the shores of Australia, they were housed in a refugee camp and given food and medical care while their refugee status was being processed. Three months later, my father and I arrived in Melbourne where we found my uncle Chinh. My father found a job at the market, and a few years later, he opened his own fruit and vegetable shop. When I was thirteen, my uncle told me about a recurring dream he had every year since we arrived, on the same date. The first of August, the day we were reunited. It was a dream that he remembered in every detail, unlike any other dream. He saw what would have happened had we not left the village. This was nothing new, we had been told about the fate of the villagers. But the dream was horrible, he saw the Kampuchean soldiers killing my parents and me in a manner that he couldn't repeat."

Guillaume had an intuition about what Lien was going to say next.

"At the end of the dream, he saw a man writing on a typewriter. He could see what he had typed, it was our story where we had fled our village and arrived in Australia."

"Was your uncle able to describe this man?"

"He was European, middle-aged, had brown hair and a moustache. My uncle had never seen him before though. But the most incredible thing was that he woke up with a tattoo on the palm of his hand. He showed it to me, an infinity symbol inside a circle. It was the same symbol that was on the typewriter. "

No doubt about it, Louis had used the typewriter, thinking he could save Lien and her parents. How could he know that only two of them would make it?

Lien finished her glass before she continued, "It was hard to dismiss it as just a dream because of the tattoo. I wondered who this man was. I had read real-life stories about guardian angels, but if that's what he was, why didn't he save my Mum as well?

When I was twenty-one, I went to Vietnam. I wanted to discover the land I was born in. Dad didn't come, he had too many bad memories. It made him very anxious, so I went with a friend and called him every day while I was there to say I was OK. It was a very strange feeling because a part of me belonged there but I was a complete stranger. Luckily Dad had always spoken to me in Vietnamese, so I didn't need a translator.

I went to my parents' village. I visited the memorial to the victims of the slaughter. It contained hundreds of skulls of the people who died, classified by age and sex. There was one of a baby and I thought that it could have been me. And the skull of a man could have been my Dad, that woman could have been my Mum. I lit a stick of incense and prayed for those who didn't have my luck. I thought about my Mum and I cried. Who knows what happened to her after she was captured by the pirates? There was a building next to the memorial with photos detailing how the villagers died, but it was too hard for me. I took one look and then walked out.

I bought a cup of tea from an old woman outside selling drinks to the tourists. She said she was the only survivor. There were no other witnesses, and the Kampuchean soldiers never acknowledged their involvement. She said that the law of karma would make sure they got what they deserved. Then she looked at me in the eyes and I wanted to run away. What if she knew my parents and saw the resemblance? I felt too guilty to tell her that my parents and I had fled the night before."

"It's not your fault though."

"I've had a good life, but she has to live with the memory of her family and friends killed before her eyes. It isn't fair."

Guillaume sighed. "There is so much injustice in the world. What about the victims, did they get what they deserved because of what they did in a past life?"

146

"I don't think so and that's why even though I was raised as a Buddhist, it doesn't mean anything to me."

"Go on, you were saying the old lady looked at you in the eyes."

"She said that there was a man who had the answers to my questions and that he lived far away but one day I would meet him. I asked her who this man was and she replied that he harvested the fruits of the womb and the vine. I'm sorry Guillaume, when you said you were an obstetrician and that your family was in the wine business, I was stunned. That's why I ran away. I know it wasn't brave of me but I didn't know what to think. I didn't believe what the old woman told me, I thought she was losing her mind. In fact I still don't know. How could you have any answers about my life?"

Guillaume didn't want to tell her now about the typewriter. He had to find Louis' diary to confirm that he had something to do with Lien's rescue. The old lady had been right, but how did she know? Guillaume didn't believe in fortune telling, but it was too much of a coincidence.

"I don't know either, Lien. All I can say is that I'm happy to have met you. And my offer still stands."

"Which offer was that?"

"To call me when you're in Paris."

"Oh yes, I forgot. Of course I will... If you give your number that is."

Guillaume gave her his card. "In fact, the sessions of the congress for the rest of the week aren't interesting. I've always wanted to visit Saint-Paul-de-Vence. Can I join you?"

Lien felt her cheeks burning, she tried to hide them with her hair. "That would be great, I've been feeling lonely on my own."

They returned to the place where they first met. The antique market had been replaced by a flower market. In the shade of striped awnings, hundreds of flowers made an explosion of colours and fragrances. Multi-coloured geraniums, intense mauve fuchsias, anemone shaped Dahlia flowers competed with each other for the attention of the buyers. A game of seduction that was difficult to resist.

During the next four days, Guillaume and Lien forgot that their time together was counted, they lived outside of time. Guillaume forgot to put on his watch, something that had never happened to him. Each minute they spent together increased the feelings they had for each other. But there were three words that were never spoken. They didn't have to be. When they looked into each other's eyes, they were there: I LOVE YOU.

No man had been able to conquer Lien's heart. Her vulnerability made her retreat at the first sign of anything that could cause her pain. The men she met didn't have the sensitivity or understanding that she was looking for.

She had found in Guillaume a soul mate. They were two souls that had a hole in their heart that they tried to fill every day. He was making the spirit of his sister live by ensuring women didn't lose their lives like she had. But she didn't know if her mother was still alive. She was torn between hoping she was and that they would one day be reunited, and hoping she hadn't had time to suffer in the hands of the pirates. Alive or not, her spirit was with her. It flowed through her hands every time she healed an animal.

When they were together, the spirits made room for their love to blossom, and it filled their hearts, the room they were in and the sky above their heads.

A chain of events that had started thirty-four years ago had allowed their love to bloom, but if any of those events were to be removed from the chain, it would break. As Guillaume was going to find out, that was an eventuality, for the past was not immutable.

Chapter Eight

26th September, Paris.

When Amélia saw that her friend was going to tour Paris with the handsome doctor, she wasn't disappointed; she relished the freedom it gave her to do some shopping on her own rather than visit the art museums that Lien had planned to see.

Guillaume discovered Paris with new eyes and understood why it was called 'the city of love', although in his condition, he would have applied that label to Kabul or Vladivostok if Lien was with him.

The French capital has always attracted people from different countries and different regions of France who bring their origins to the recipe that makes Paris unique. The south-west of France wasn't on Lien's itinerary, but the Canal Saint-Martin with its *pétanque* players gave her a taste of the Canal Du Midi. The Market on Place Saint-Paul brought together produce from the regions of France. Guillaume cooked lunch with the ingredients they had bought: slices of *pain de campagne* with saucisson from Lyon were followed by chicken breasts from Bresse with Normandy fresh cream and Paris champignons. Not a single crumb was left of the tarte Tatin, the upside down caramelised apple tart that Guillaume had mastered to perfection. Guillaume and Lien sat down on the sofa; Louis' diary was on the table, Guillaume had found it tucked away in a bookshelf, it had confirmed what Guillaume thought. He said, "There's something I want to show you."

"What is it?"

"Something to do with that old woman you saw in your parents' village. She was right, I do have some answers. I didn't tell you before because I wanted to be sure."

"It sounds very interesting."

"Yes, but don't get your hopes up, it's probably not what you expected."

"I didn't know what to expect anyway."

"This is my grandfather's diary; he made an amazing discovery. You're going to find this hard to believe, but I can assure you it's true. The typewriter your uncle saw in his dreams exists, and it can be used to change a person's past."

Lien didn't show any reaction, she was taking in the information, waiting for Guillaume to continue.

"This typewriter has a long history. It was made in 1868 in a little village near Nantes, in the north-west of France, and brought to Laos by a French missionary. It was stolen by the Japanese during their occupation of that country in World War Two. Thirty years later, my grandfather Louis went to Japan to sell some Burgundy wines. One of his customers was the soldier who had stolen the typewriter and he offered it to him. He had no use for the typewriter with its western letters, but thought Louis could do something with it. It was his was way of thanking Louis for introducing French wines to him. It was a unique piece, with its SUTHCI keyboard layout and decorated keys. That's what Louis thought, but he found out that it was unique for an entirely different reason.

After Japan, Louis went to Melbourne. One of his clients supplied wines to restaurants in the south eastern suburbs of the city. He took Louis to your uncle Chinh's restaurant, Indochine."

"But how did you know that it was my uncle's restaurant?"

"I'll come to that in a moment. Louis was a gourmet and he wrote in his diary how much he enjoyed that meal. He asked to see the chef to congratulate him and as he spoke, he saw in your uncle's eyes that he had lost someone close and dear to him."

"When was it?"

Guillaume opened the diary and searched for the day Louis was in Melbourne. "First of August, 1978."

Lien's head tilted to the side and she ran her hands through her hair. "But it's the date we found uncle Chinh. I know the date because we celebrate the anniversary of our reunion with him every year."

"Yes, but this is in an alternate reality, where your Dad and you didn't make it. Let me continue and it will make sense..." He paused and then said, "I hope. Louis woke up during the night and saw that the keys of the typewriter were glowing. It happens when it's ready to give you a vision. I've experienced it myself, but it's a story for another time. The light became so bright that he closed his eyes. He saw a man's life flash before his eyes; he didn't know it at the time, but it was your uncle Chinh's." Guillaume took the typewritten sheets that were folded inside the diary and gave them to Lien. "He typed what he saw; I'll let you read it,"

Lien unfolded the sheets and looked at Guillaume. He nodded to her and she started reading.

His name was Chinh. He was born in Ba Chúc, a village in southern Vietnam. He was married to Tham, a girl from his village, and they had a daughter called Mai.

He said to Tham, "My friend Dien was sent to a re-education camp because he worked for the US army during the war. I've heard terrible stories about those camps, I may never see him again. The government knows I worked for the US army too, I could be next."

"What are we going to do?"

"We have to leave the country. I've found a fishing boat that could take us to Australia. It leaves next week."

"But Chinh, it's so sudden. What will we do when we get there?"

"I'm going to convert the money the US army gave me into gold. I'll find work there, it's a land of opportunity. I could even open a restaurant." I'll have to sew the gold inside my trousers, he thought. If we get attacked by pirates, they won't see it, but I better not tell Tham, she would be too worried.

The next day, he went to see his brother Duong and informed him of his plan. "Come with us," he said, "there's room in the boat for you, Kim and Lien."

"Why take a risk? We have a good life here."

"The army will find you and send you to a re-education camp."

"What have I done?"

"Nothing, but you're my brother, it might be a sufficient reason for them. They are crazy with revenge."

"They'll never think of coming to get me in Ba Chúc. You worked in Saigon, that was the most dangerous place to be."

Chinh said goodbye to his brother, not knowing if he would ever see him again..

They landed in Australia and were offered a place in a migrant hostel in Springvale, a suburb of Melbourne, with the promise of a permanent visa.

"I wish Duong and his family were here," Chinh said. "They could have a good life like us. I wrote to him to tell him that we made it, thinking that it could make him change his mind, but when I went to the post office, they said that I couldn't send it because of the sanctions against the new regime."

"That's a shame, I hope he's still OK."

"There's no way of knowing; those sanctions are useless anyway, the regime will keep doing whatever they want. In four weeks, it will be the third anniversary of the end of the war, but it won't be a happy occasion for everyone. The war is still claiming lives, people are dying in the re-education camps. Oh, when will it end?"

"Louis wrote in his diary that he could not only see what Chinh was seeing but also feel what he was feeling. He had no doubt that what he saw was real, but he didn't understand why he had been given this vision. Could it have something to do with the Vietnamese restaurant he had dined in the night before? It could have been a coincidence, there were lots of Vietnamese restaurants in Springvale. The next day, Louis called his client. He was a regular of the restaurant and he confirmed that the chef's name was Chinh. It could have been another coincidence, Chinh was a common Vietnamese name. Then he remembered the name of the village. He had heard about Ba Chúc in the news; it had been wiped out by the Kampuchean soldiers but he couldn't remember the date. He re-read what he had typed; the story ended one month before Reunification day, which is the 30th of April. Louis called the archive department of The Age and he got confirmation of what he feared. The story that he had typed had stopped before the massacre which happened on the 18th of April. When he saw your uncle, the distress he had seen in his eyes was that of having lost his brother."

"But how can this be true? That's not what happened!"

"That's right. Louis wondered why the story hadn't continued until the present, it was incomplete. He looked at the typewriter and waited for another vision. It didn't come and the keys were no longer glowing. Suddenly a light came from the back of the typewriter and the letters of Caveat Emendator appeared on the ceiling."

"What does it mean?"

"Corrector Beware in Latin, which Louis didn't know. The feeling that he hadn't been given this story for nothing remained. He knew the ending and was affected by it. Then he tried to type a different continuation; it didn't work the first time because he couldn't force your father to do something he didn't want. The only thing he could do was to give him a reason to change his mind. After a few tries, he found something that the typewriter let him write. Here it is."

Guillaume gave Lien the other sheet that Louis had typed:

"Hello," said Vinh, a fellow Vietnamese who had arrived in the hostel a month before Chinh. "I've heard that you're from near the border with Kampuchea."

"Yes, I'm from Ba Chúc," Chinh said.

"Do you still have family there?"

"Yes, my brother, but I haven't found of way of contacting him to tell him he can come."

"I have a cousin in Kampuchea; he's not far from Ba Chúc and he communicates with Vietnamese folks with his carrier pigeon. He could pass on a message to your brother if you send it to him."

Chinh laughed and said, "That would be great, I'll write the message now." He went to his room and took a sheet of paper and a pen.

'Dear Brother,

Our trip was a bit rough as we were attacked by pirates, but we made it to Australia. All you need to do is to hide your valuables and keep some to give to them. We are now in a migrant hostel and I'm going to open a restaurant and cook mum's recipes. Australia is a land of peace and freedom. You are not as safe as you think in Ba Chúc. One day the army will get you. I hope it won't happen, but hope isn't enough. You have to make your destiny, not wait for someone else to make it for you. I know you disapproved of me deserting my country and risking my life and the life of Mai and Tham, but believe me, you will not regret it if you join us. I will look after you little brother.'

Guillaume smiled. "You know the rest of the story."

"Yes, that is what happened; Dad told me that he got a letter from his brother in Australia. He was still hesitating to leave because I was a little baby, but Mum convinced him. She thought it was riskier to stay in Ba Chúc where Dad could be taken to a re-education camp than to travel on a fishing boat to Australia. If Chinh had made it, they could too. When I think that she was the one to push my Dad to go and she didn't make it. She sacrificed herself so that we could have a better life."

"Your mum was courageous."

"But I can't believe your grandfather used the typewriter to change the past."

"Louis didn't believe it either at first, but a strange thing happened. That night, he had a dream where his client took him to Indochine and he saw your uncle, but when he woke up, he had no memory of what he had done that evening, just this dream. He was confused, so he asked his client to remind him of the name of the restaurant they went to two days ago. He said it was the Saltimbocca. Then Louis asked him if he'd heard of Indochine. He replied was that it was one of his favourites, but when he had called to reserve a table, he was told that it was closed because the chef was celebrating his reunion with his brother.

Louis opened his diary and saw that in the entry for that day, they had gone to Indochine. It didn't make sense. He never wrote his dreams in his diary. Then he remembered that he had called the archive department of The Age the day after having typed the first part of the story. The number of victims was reported as 3160. He called again to check. He wanted to convince himself that nothing had changed, but that's not what happened. The number of victims was 3157."

"A difference of three. The first number included my parents and me, the second number didn't. This is so weird, and yet everything corresponds. The man my uncle saw in his dream about the alternate reality where my parents and I were massacred was your grandfather."

"That's how the typewriter works; it gives a vision of what would have happened if the person's life hadn't been changed, and it erases the alternate reality from the writer's memory. Louis couldn't remember going to Indochine; because of the change he made, it didn't happen. I know this because I've had the same experience twice."

"Do you still have the typewriter?"

"I've put it a bank safe because someone's tried to steal it. I don't know who it is but he is armed and dangerous. Imagine what it could do if it fell in the wrong hands."

"Yes, but I would really like to see it. It means a lot to me. If it wasn't for the typewriter and of course your grandfather, I would be dead, a statistic of history, the youngest victim of that massacre."

"There isn't much time, the bank closes in an hour."

"It doesn't matter, I just want to see it, I won't be long."

Guillaume and Lien rushed to the bank; the manager in charge of the vault room asked them to be quick, because they only had forty-five minutes.

"It's beautiful," Lien said as Guillaume put the typewriter on the table.

The keys glowed; Lien closed her eyes and started typing.

His name was Guillaume; he was born in 1980 in Gevrey-Saint-André.

He cried when his sister Bénédicte moved out of the house to study in Paris when he was five.

"I'll miss you Béné," Guillaume said.

"Don't worry Billy, I'll come back on the week-ends to see you. It's not far by train." Bénédicte said.

At the dinner table that winter, Marie-Ange asked, "Are you making friends at uni?"

"It's hard, everyone stays in their own group, Africans with other Africans, Parisians with other Parisians and Bretons with other Bretons. But I don't mind; all the girls are interested in is going out, drinking and sleeping with boys," Bénédicte replied.

"And no boyfriend on the horizon?" Christophe asked with a touch of worry in his voice.

"Maybe."

"Tell us more," Marie-Ange said.

"I met a boy two weeks ago; his name is Pathana, he's from a little village in Laos. He got a scholarship from the French department of education, otherwise his parents wouldn't have been able to send him here. His country is very poor and has an abundance of children, but not enough teachers to educate them. This is the first time he's been out of his country. The furthest he had been from his village was Vientiane, the capital city, where he went to high school."

"How is he finding life in Paris?"

"He was surprised that people rushed from one place to another, never taking the time to say hello to each other. He doesn't understand how people who live with fine food, beautiful art and architecture can be so rude. He's tried to strike conversations with other students, but he hasn't had any success."

"How's his French?"

"Quite good, he learnt it at high school. He's got a little accent, it's so cute. He knows a lot about France, he's got one of those little plastic maps with the rivers and cities, like the one you had, Dad."

Christophe smiled and Bénédicte continued. "He's here with his friends. They live very simply. They save their allowance for their parents, but on Pathana's birthday, they treated him to a real French restaurant. Pathana loved the Boeuf Bourguignon but the Steak Tartare made his friends sick. The next day, they didn't go to class and he was on his own, so I went to speak to him."

"How did it go?" Marie-Ange asked.

"We went for a coffee and we spent the afternoon together. It was great; he's kind and modest, not like the boys here."

The next month, Bénédicte introduced Pathana to her family.

"I'm very happy to meet you, Bénédicte has spoken a lot about you and especially Guillaume." He bent down and said to Guillaume, "She told me you can already read a book."

"Yes, she taught me to read," Guillaume said.

"I'm sure she will make a great teacher." He straightened himself and said to Marie-Ange and Christophe, "In our country, teachers are respected and we need more, education is the only way to get our children out of poverty."

After their graduation, Pathana and Bénédicte married.

"Marriage is a covenant, not just like a contract," the priest said, "but in the sense of a commitment of love given and received, of total sharing of life. The object of this covenant is the happiness of the other and the happiness of the one who loves. Remember the words of our Lord from the gospel of Saint John. 'This is my commandment, that you love one another as I have loved you. There is no greater love than to lay down your life for your friends.' Let us remember that to love is to want the happiness of the other."

Guillaume was sad because he knew that Bénédicte and Pathana were going to go to the other side of the world. Guillaume loved his sister and wanted her happiness, but it was a heavy price to pay. Couldn't they have stayed? There are lots of children to teach here. He dreamed of the day he was going to board a plane to Laos to see her.

Lien looked at the sheets she had typed and said, "I saw your life flashing before my eyes until your sister's wedding. You hadn't mentioned her, is she still in Laos?"

Guillaume rubbed his right eye and swallowed.

Lien asked, "What's wrong Guillaume? Did something happen to her?"

"Yes, she died there, giving birth to her first child."

"I'm sorry."

"The worst thing is that we were left with nothing to grieve over. Her ashes were scattered in the river Mekong the next day and we were never able to contact Pathana. All we had left were our memories of what a wonderful person she was and her paintings."

Before she could say something to Guillaume, the security guard came in and said, "I'm sorry but the bank is closing, you have to close your safe now."

Guillaume looked at Lien and the typewriter. This was the chance he had been waiting for. Lien could save Bénédicte.

"I will take this with me, just give me the paperwork to sign," Guillaume said to the guard.

"But isn't the typewriter safer here?" Lien said.

"There's no time to lose, I'll take it home and you can change the rest the story. I'll put it back in the safe tomorrow."

Lien didn't have time to reply, Guillaume had signed the form and they were leaving the bank with the typewriter.

161

Guillaume and Lien walked briskly to the apartment, his jaw was clenched and he was sweating.

When they arrived, Guillaume said, "While we're waiting for Caveat Emendator to be projected on the ceiling, we have to think about the way that she is going to be saved. You need to stop her from going to Laos."

"How can I do that? You said that the typewriter couldn't interfere with someone's mind."

"If there was a war in Laos, they wouldn't want to go there."

"But you don't want thousands of people to be killed in a war."

"No, of course not."

"The Laotian embassy could refuse Bénédicte's visa."

"Yes, that could work, but for how long?"

The front door opened and Sylvie walked in the room. She said, "Hi Guillaume, why have you taken the typewriter out of the safe, it's a bit risky, isn't it?"

"Hi Sylvie. I hadn't had time to tell you—I found Louis' diary. He used the typewriter to save Lien and her father. I took her to the bank to see it and she typed my story until Bénédicte's wedding. Do you realise what this means? Lien can stop her from going to Laos and losing her life."

Sylvie's face darkened. "Wait! You have to be careful, changing the past can have unpredictable consequences. Remember Sophie? I was thinking about her today. I found her funeral notice when I googled her, she died in a car accident a year ago. By saving her mother, you killed her."

Guillaume raised his voice. "How can you say that? The fact that she died in a car accident has nothing to do with the changes I made to her life."

"But it does, because of the change you made, she had a completely different life; probably a better one that allowed her to buy a car and that's what killed her."

Lien interrupted the conversation. "Your grandfather tried to save the three of us but only my father and I made it. I don't know what's better, being dead or living the rest of my life separated from my mother, thinking that she's a slave to the pirates. Who knows? Who are we to decide what's better? This typewriter makes you like God, changing the lives of humans. But He doesn't control everything either."

"I'm sorry Lien," Guillaume said. "My parents and I have been through hell since Bénédicte died, and I would do anything to take the pain away. When I found that the typewriter could change the past, I thought I could use it to save Bénédicte, but the inventor put some restrictions on how the typewriter can be used after a person he had saved killed his brother. I lost hope, but when I met you, I had no idea that the typewriter would give you a vision of my life."

"Look Guillaume, I know it's hard for you. I share your pain."

"It must be even harder for you, not knowing what happened to your mother."

"I've lived my life the way I thought she would have liked me to live, with love, honour and courage. I have no memories of her, but I believe that wherever she is, she protects me. Every night before I go to sleep, I speak to her, I tell her what I've done and how I feel."

Guillaume wished he could tell her about what happened to her mother, but he hadn't had any visions about Lien's life, which was unusual.

He thought about Claire; she hadn't known her mother either, but unlike Lien, she knew that her mother had passed away. Guillaume had no evidence that Bénédicte was dead, but if she wasn't, she would have tried to contact her family. The idea that she was being held captive by Laotian bandits came back to haunt him as he thought of Lien's mother at the hands of Thai pirates. It was another thing they had in common—a loved one lost without a trace.

Lien turned her head to look at the typewriter and Guillaume and Sylvie followed her gaze. The keys were glowing again, of a green light that filled the room. The silence was broken by a melody, as if an invisible hand was striking invisible crystal glasses delicately. A message appeared on the sheet of paper that had stayed there, waiting to be filled.

Where the triad of nations that supply dragon chasers with their poison meet, the mother river flows and I wait for you Billy. My thread hasn't been woven into the tapestry of lives gone by, the time hasn't come yet. Come and we will be together again. Take the fish with you, it will show you the way. But beware of the evil man, guard it with your life.

Guillaume, Lien and Sylvie waited for more to come, but the keys stopped glowing. Guillaume took the sheet and read the message aloud. He scratched his head and read it again.

"Do you have any idea what it means?" Lien asked.

"A dragon chaser is a heroin addict," Sylvie said.

"The triad of nations that supply heroin must be a reference to the golden triangle. Laos, Burma and Thailand," Guillaume said.

"The mother river is what the Thai and the Lao call the Mekong," Lien added. "But what about the thread?"

"The druid I saw in the cave," Guillaume replied. "He said that each life was a thread waiting to be woven into the tapestry of lives gone by, and that there was a thread that wasn't where I thought it was."

"Do you think he has something to do with this message?" Sylvie asked.

"He said that previous lives determined your destiny, and it had seemed odd to me because it sounded like karma, but the three countries are Buddhist, so it doesn't seem so strange now."

"And who is Billy?"

"It's what Bénédicte called me, and she was the only one to do that. My parents didn't like it and my friends only called me Guillaume."

Guillaume, Sylvie and Lien looked at each other. They had reached the same conclusion but didn't dare say it aloud. Lien broke the silence. "Guillaume, I think it means your sister is still alive in Laos and the typewriter has transmitted a message from her."

"If she's still alive, then her thread isn't in the tapestry of lives gone by," Sylvie said.

Guillaume felt his legs shaking; he sat down and read the message silently, his eyes widening. He hesitated for a moment and said, "Everything concurs with that conclusion, except the style of the message. It's not how she speaks or writes."

"And what about the fish?" Sylvie asked.

"It's a reference to the first six letters on the keyboard of the typewriter, I, C, H, T, U and S. ICHTHUS is the ancient Greek word for fish. 'Guard it with your life' is not a vain statement. Someone knows about the typewriter and is ready to kill to get it."

"But if it's from Bénédicte, how can she know about the typewriter?"

"Her captors probably do, they must have asked her to send the message. She must be in big trouble. I remember thinking that she had been kidnapped by Laotian bandits and that they were keeping her hostage. It doesn't seem so far-fetched now."

"Do you think it's a trap?"

Guillaume laughed nervously. "It doesn't matter. If there's a possibility that Bénédicte is still alive, it's worth taking the risk. I'm going to go to Laos to look for her. If her captors are after the typewriter, they can have it."

"I'm coming with you." Sylvie said.

"No way, it's too dangerous for a—"

"A girl, is that what you were going to say? Do I have to remind you that it's thanks to me and my guitar that you still have the typewriter? Besides, you're going to need all the help you can get if you have to rescue her from a gang of bandits."

"Sorry Sylvie, I didn't mean that. But anything was to happen to you, I would never forgive myself."

"You're not forcing me, I'm coming of my own free will, so whatever happens, you're not to blame."

"Thanks Sylvie, you're right, I'll feel a lot better if I'm not on my own."

"I'll leave you two alone, I'm going to do some research on visas and flights."

After Sylvie had left, Lien sat next to Guillaume. She took his hand and said, "We've only got one day left together and I wanted to tell you that my life will never be the same now that I've met you. I never thought I would ever meet a man with your sensitivity and generosity. Not only that, but you're the grandson of the man who saved my Dad and me. Our lives were connected from the start, our meeting was bound to happen."

"I never thought I would ever say this, but it does look like we were destined to meet each other. I fell in love with you the first time we met, but I thought it was such a fluke, like winning the lottery—it felt unreal. But that was before I knew Louis had saved you and if it wasn't for that, I would never have known that my sister was still alive. The days we spent together were magical and I will never forget them, nor will I forget you."

Lien put her head on Guillaume's chest and felt his heart beat for her.

"Our paths have crossed," Guillaume continued, "but now we have to resume the course of our lives. They have been made richer by the love that has filled our hearts. We knew our time was counted right from the start and it made it more precious and intense."

Guillaume paused and said, "Unless there was a way we could be together.'

Lien raised her head and waited for Guillaume to continue.

"There are many places where there are Doctors Without Borders and Veterinarians Without Borders—"

"I'm sorry Guillaume, but I can't leave Australia. It's my duty to look after my father. After what he's been through, I can't abandon him, it would be the end of him."

Guillaume was about to say something, but Lien went on to say with a broken voice, "I want you to know Guillaume—my heart is yours for ever, I will never love another man, and if one day you felt your time with Doctors Without Borders was up and you wanted to settle down, you could start a new life in Australia with me. The country has a shortage of doctors, you would be able to work there."

Guillaume stroked her face and said, "My heart is yours too Lien. I don't know if our lives will cross again, nor do I know what I will find in Laos. Anything is possible. I could lose my life trying to save Bénédicte, but if I do, I will be in peace because I have found love."

Lien shook her head. "Don't say that, I don't want to lose you, even if you're far away. When you go to Laos, you will see the mother river. It's the river where my parents swam and fished, the same river that you thought had carried the ashes of your sister to the sea. It links our lives together. Take a handful of rice and throw it in the river for protection. It's an old superstition that my father believes in, he did that before we left. The fact that my mother didn't make it didn't change his belief; he said he should have thrown more rice, but who knows? I don't usually believe in this sort of thing, but then again, I would never have believed the past could be changed with a typewriter. Even if you think this is silly, do it for me."

"I will, my love." Guillaume cupped her face in his hands and kissed her softly.

Our destinies are connected; they form an intricate but fragile web that is woven every day when new strands link our lives with other lives. The weaver is the only one who can see how a change in one life affects the lives that it is connected with. Guillaume, Lien, Sylvie, the Master, Aaron, Louis and Bénédicte—seven destinies, seven hundred and twenty possible connections, but only those who are already dead need not fear for their lives.

Chapter Nine

5th October, Vientiane Airport, Laos.

Aaron looked at the arrival board; flight 8764 from Paris was expected to land in twenty-two minutes. It had been easy to arrange his trip to Vientiane. He had told his boss that he was following some leads there. It was plausible, Laos and Russia had close ties since the victory of the communists in Laos. He had monitored Guillaume's broadband connection and knew when he was landing and where he was staying. Guillaume and Sylvie were going to find some delays in retrieving their luggage. Aaron had bribed the man in charge of baggage handling operations. Men were the same in developing countries, you could always get what you wanted if you paid the price. The rainy season was in its last month; Arron hated this weather, the humidity made his clothes cling to his skin.

He went to the baggage handling area where he opened Guillaume and Sylvie's luggage. They had packed their necessities in backpacks, but Guillaume had taken the typewriter with him on the plane. Aaron inserted a tracking device and a microphone in each backpack and put them back with the others. He was patient. He was going to wait until they were in a quiet place and if they opposed any resistance, he would have no hesitation in using his gun.

Aaron looked like a typical backpacker, with his long hair, dirty jeans and a T-shirt with the effigy of Che Guevara. From now on, he was going to follow them closely. He was on the same flight to Ban Houayxay, a town in the north-east of

169

the country, and he was going to stay at the same guest house.

After Guillaume and Sylvie had checked in at the guest house in Ban Houayxay, they went to a nearby restaurant. They ate their *laab*, a dish with chopped meat and spices served with sticky rice.

"It's hard to believe that four days ago I was in Paris trying to find a way to stop Bénédicte from going to Laos, and now I'm looking for her," Guillaume said. "I haven't had time to get used to the idea that she may be still alive."

"I don't want to put you off, but I hope this isn't a wild goose chase."

"At the very least, I'm hoping to have some answers. When my parents came to Laos, they didn't find any trace of Pathana; his parents thought he was still in France, and they hadn't heard of his brother since he had left the village to join a Buddhist temple. He hadn't told them where the temple was; my parents visited a few temples in the region, but no one had heard of Keona. They wrote to every Buddhist temple in Laos after they came back from their trip, but the result was the same."

Sylvie lit a cigarette and looked at the other guests. Most were backpackers enjoying a country that was not spoilt by progress. The pace of life was as slow as the Mekong river. Life remained the same. The only hint of the twenty-first century was the "Free Wi-Fi" sign in the lobby. Laotians were relaxed and welcomed tourists as if they were family.

"I have this strange feeling, like we're being watched. I'm beginning to act like a paranoiac, looking over my shoulder all the time. I know it's silly though. I mean, how could the burglar track us all the way here?"

"I think he's more than a burglar; he knows a lot. He's been to the apartment twice when I wasn't there, he knew Louis had planned to go to New Orleans. If he's that determined to get the typewriter, he could have found a way to follow us here."

Sylvie puffed on her cigarette nervously. "Stop it, you're scaring me!"

"You should've brought your guitar, it could come in handy."

"It's not funny, that guy nearly killed me! I still have nightmares about it. If he succeeds this time, he'll just bury our bodies in the jungle where no one will ever find us. The perfect crime."

Guillaume shuddered. "Now you're the one scaring me." He wiped his lips with a serviette. "I really wonder what he wants to do with the typewriter."

"I don't know, maybe he spent time in jail and wants to change the past so he doesn't get caught."

They were silent for a while, looking for calm in the peaceful flowing of the mighty Mekong River.

"The mother river," Guillaume said. "If Bénédicte is still alive, it means I've spent twenty-two years believing that her ashes were scattered on this river. But it's a long time for her to be in captivity, I can't imagine being locked up for so long."

"Neither can I, but who can her captors be?"

"I have no idea, I really don't know what to expect. In the best case, we exchange the typewriter for Bénédicte's freedom and we all go home. I don't want to think about the worst case."

"But what are they going to do with it?"

"Whatever it is, I can't see how it concerns us."

"Unless what the druid said about the cosmic order is true."

"Yes, but he said that there were evil forces threatening to destroy it and the message mentioned an evil man, it must be the burglar."

"That would make Bénédicte's captors the good guys, it doesn't make sense."

"Whoever they are, they must know about Émile Vattier, which means that he spoke to someone about the typewriter while he was here."

"I'll do a search on French missions in Laos." Sylvie took her phone out of her pocket. "There's only one page. Let me see. At that time, the missionaries that were evangelising Laos were based in Nakon Phanom. It's a village on the Thai side of the Mekong, but it's a long way from here. After the Indochina war, the missionaries left and appointed local bishops to look after their flock."

"The common element between this village, the place indicated by the typewriter and where Bénédicte lived is the Mekong river."

"This place seems peaceful, and yet we're near the golden triangle."

"I wish I was in peace myself." Guillaume took the typewriter out of his bag and put it on the table. It remained silent. Guillaume ordered another bottle of wine.

"Don't drink too much, you'll need to have a clear head tomorrow."

"You're right, I was trying to calm my nerves, but it's going to take a lot more."

After Sylvie had gone to her room, Guillaume walked to the river bank. He threw the rice than Lien had given him in the river. A group of children were playing nearby; a woman who had seen Guillaume, presumably their mother, clasped her hands and bowed to him. Guillaume greeted her back and watched her throw some rice. It could have fed her family, but the Mekong was part of her family, it was the mother river, loved and respected by its children. Nothing was taken for granted here.

Anxiety, heat and mosquitoes conspired to keep Guillaume and Sylvie awake during the night, and they succeeded. The two friends were the first to eat breakfast at the guest house.

"They certainly know how to make good baguettes here," Sylvie said, "it's a pity they don't have Nutella."

"That's a good legacy the French colonials left behind. If they had stayed longer, they could have built more roads and train tracks. The only way to reach our destination is by boat."

"Suits me," Sylvie said laconically. She had never been afraid of the unknown. She thrived on it. New experiences, new sensations, new people. It was as though she was running away from familiarity. She had been running away from a part of herself. The part she hated, the part that hurt, that nothing could soothe. She had never thought about it, it was an instinctive reaction. It had numbed her pain. But now, it felt like she had run into a brick wall. She couldn't escape any more, she had to confront her demons. The time had come to tell Guillaume the truth, but she put it off again. What difference was another day going to make?

After breakfast, Guillaume and Sylvie checked out of the guest house and went to the jetty to see if they could find a boat to the place indicated by the typewriter. There was no shortage of boats travelling downstream to Luang Prabang, but their destination was upstream. They took a ferry to the Thai village of Chiang Khong on the other side of the river, where they boarded a speed boat to Tung Luang Chalerm Phrakiat, on the Thai side of the junction between the three countries.

When they reached their destination, it was raining. Thick, heavy warm water poured from the skies. Guillaume and Sylvie found shelter in a bar next to the opium museum and drank a can of Coke while they waited. Ten minutes later the rain stopped.

"We've assumed all along that the place we're going to is in Laos but it could be in Burma or Thailand," Sylvie said.

"We'll see if the typewriter gives us some directions, but I want to find a quiet place, I don't want anyone to see it."

They walked out of the bar and stopped to look at a ten metre golden statue of Buddha guarded by two elephants. Tourists were taking photos and posing in front of the elephants.

"It's funny how they've put this giant Buddha so close to the opium museum."

"I wonder if they ever thought opium as a shortcut to reaching Nirvana."

"More like a way of reaching hell," Sylvie said, thinking of a friend she had lost from a heroin overdose.

They walked until they found a place away from prying eyes. Guillaume looked hesitantly at the sky before taking the typewriter out of his bag. He inserted the crystal in the back and waited. He turned it ninety degrees to the right and waited again. It stayed silent. The third time was conclusive.

"This is the moment of truth."

Guillaume crossed his arms and waited for the typewriter to deliver its message; it was sluggish, as if it was slowed down by the heat.

Across the mother river, the crystal will guide you.

Have faith little brother, it is the time and place for our

destinies to be reunited.

"How are we going to cross?" Sylvie asked.

Guillaume looked through his binoculars. "There aren't many bridges around here, not that there's any reason to build one. There are just three houses huddled together on the other side, and beyond them, a hilly forest. We'll have to ask for a boat to take us there."

Sylvie and Guillaume walked to a man who was sitting on a crate and smoking near a small boat.

After Guillaume's attempts to ask to cross the river in French and English failed, he resorted to gesticulating.

Guillaume and Sylvie didn't understand his reply but the look on his face didn't need translating. He was terrified of what was on the other side. The bank note Guillaume showed him didn't dissipate his fear, but two more of the same persuaded him to sell his boat.

Guillaume put the boat in the water and Sylvie climbed aboard. The current was strong. They rowed vigorously to get across the river. Guillaume secured the boat with a rope, hoping that it would still be there when they came back.

The bright colours, the smell of incense, the chanting and the gongs that they had left gave way to an empty and lifeless silence. The houses looked as though their occupants had fled in a hurry. Sylvie grabbed Guillaume's hand and squeezed it.

"Guillaume, if we don't make it, there's something I need to tell you."

"Don't be silly, we'll be fine. The druid said this crystal was a protection. He didn't say our destiny was to perish on the bank of the Mekong like my sister supposedly did," Guillaume said with a soothing voice. "Everyone's gone, but where to?"

Sylvie took a sip of water and looked at the crystal Guillaume was holding in front of his eyes. He lowered it and then raised it again. "I can see a purple light coming from that hill straight ahead, over there."

"I hope we get to wherever we're supposed to go before it gets dark."

"We'll pitch our tents if we have to."

The two friends walked in silence, slowed down by the weight of their backpacks. Guillaume carried the typewriter and food, Sylvie had the tent and water. When they reached the forest, they found a path that had been cut through the trees; crystals were strewn on the ground, showing the way. The slope of the hill slowed them down further. After two hours which felt like twice as long, they took a welcome break.

"I have a feeling of déjà vu, but this time I would be very surprised if I found a druid," Guillaume said.

"You never know, we may not have had our full share of surprises yet."

"We've made good progress, if our destination is at the top of the hill, we should be there soon."

Another hour later, Guillaume stopped. "Do you hear that?"

"What?"

"It sounds like gongs."

"Yes you're right, it could a temple."

"It's unusual, Buddhist temples are usually in the middle of towns and villages so they can be fed by the community."

Sylvie thought of the monastery that was a few kilometres from Gevrey-Saint-André. The monks had taken a vow of silence and were never seen, nor did they need to be. They were completely self-sufficient, growing their own fruits and vegetables, milking their goats and cows, even making their own paper.

"It's nearly dusk, do you think we could stay there for the night? It would be better than the tent."

"Unless it's our destination."

"Do you think Bénédicte is being held hostage by Buddhist monks? I thought Buddhists were non-violent."

"Maybe she's there of her own accord."

"Why would she have pretended to be dead then?"

Guillaume shrugged. "There's only one way to find out."

Sylvie bit her nails. The jungle was hot, but she felt a chill inside, it made her teeth chatter. *This is it, there's no turning back now.* She reached for the crystal that was inside her pocket, a gift from Clémentine who believed in the healing power of crystals. According to her, they could balance your chakras, the seven centres of vital energy described in Hindu and Buddhist traditions. She had given Sylvie a rose quartz crystal before she left, explaining that pink was the colour of love and harmony, ideal for the heart chakra. She put it near her heart, but it didn't slow it down. She wished she could hold the crystal that the druid gave Guillaume, it would be more efficient.

They kept walking until they reached a clearing. A wooden two-metre high fence gave no indication of what was inside. Guillaume and Sylvie didn't have time to think about how to make their presence known. The gate opened as soon as they were in front of it, and two young men walked towards them. Their head was shaven and they wore purple silk robes. They clasped their hands and bowed. Guillaume and Sylvie did the same. They obeyed the two men who gestured to follow them, respecting the heavy silence that had replaced the sound of the gongs. A third man came towards them carrying a torch. They entered a large wooden building and the three men led Guillaume to a room and Sylvie to an adjoining room. A candle on a wooden table gave enough light to see that there was some food in a bowl and a pitcher of water, and a reed matt on the floor. As soon as the men left, Sylvie knocked softly on Guillaume's door.

"What do we do now?"

"Eat, drink and sleep. Tomorrow is another day."

"Is that all? Don't you want to find out where we are?"

"What can we do? It's dark and the only living beings we have seen didn't say a word."

"Let's see if the typewriter has anything to say to us."

Guillaume took it out of his bag. It hummed and wrote the word Welcome.

"It looks like we've arrived."

Sylvie was about to say something when Guillaume said, "I don't know about you but I'm so tired that I could fall asleep anywhere, even on this matt. See you tomorrow."

Sylvie went back to her room.

I don't know how he can be so calm, this matt's as hard as a plank, I'm never going to fall asleep.

But exhaustion won over the dread that filled Sylvie's mind, and she fell asleep minutes after she lied down.

Guillaume opened his eyes and looked at his watch. It was 6:00 AM. The gong sounded like it was in his room. He splashed some water on his face and went to see Sylvie who was still lying down.

"Have you seen what time it is? These people have no mercy! Ah, the alarm bell has stopped, I'll go back to sleep."

The sound of chanting stopped Sylvie's plan from being realised.

"Why don't you join them instead of staying here and listening to me complaining?"

"No thanks, I'll wait for our host to come to us, whenever that may be."

Guillaume and Sylvie didn't have to wait long, five minutes after the chanting stopped, there was a knock on the door. Guillaume opened and the two men that they saw yesterday smiled at him. The older one said in impeccable French, "I hope you had a pleasant night."

"Good thank you," replied Guillaume, surprised that the man spoke.

"We are only permitted to speak between sunrise and sunset. Please come now, the Master is expecting you."

"The Master?"

"He is our spiritual leader, a fountain of wisdom that quenches our thirst and a beacon that shows us the way to enlightenment."

"I can't wait to meet him," Guillaume said wryly.

The two men led Guillaume and Sylvie to a room that nothing distinguished from the others, apart from its size and the bookshelves that lined the walls. The Master was sitting on the floor in the lotus position and he invited his guests to do likewise.

"Guillaume, by coming here, you have fulfilled your destiny to stop evil forces from destroying the cosmic order."

Guillaume looked at the Master. He looked nothing like the man who uttered the same words with the same voice two months ago, but he had the same pendant that the druid had.

"You are right, we have met before, although I looked much older. Sylvie didn't see me because I only projected my image to speak to you."

He paused and looked at Sylvie. His piercing eyes made her uncomfortable. He turned to Guillaume. "You are impatient to see Bénédicte. It's the only reason you have come here. You thought she was dead and that you could redeem her death by saving other women. You've lived your life on a lie, like many others. Illusions of the senses and the ego are no different. Men cling to their illusions, some are ready to die for them. They imprison themselves and throw away the key. It's their choice of course, they do it willingly."

Guillaume didn't know what to say.

"You are wondering when I am going to stop reading your thoughts," the Master continued. "I will explain to you shortly how I can see what is happening in the next room and on the other side of the earth, what has already happened and what will happen. Now stop thinking about your sister. She has been my guest and you will see her once you have handed over the Vidhi-Vikalpaka, or transformer of destinies as you say in your language. This contraption could destroy the universe if it fell in the wrong hands. It is my mission to stop this annihilation."

The Master poured some tea into three wooden cups and gave one to Guillaume and the second one to Sylvie. He took a sip from his cup and continued. "You wonder who I am to call myself Master and to appoint myself saviour of the universe. My family has been Christian through the generations since they were converted by Émile Vattier. I won't repeat what you already know about this person. I was baptised, received what you call an education at a missionary school. Reading, writing, mathematics, catechism, my young mind soaked it up like a sponge. I believed what I was told and I thought that following the appropriate rites and saying the right prayers would save me from hell. I was promised paradise and did everything I could to earn my right of entry.

This changed the day my father was killed in front of me when he stepped on a mine. I was twenty-one. The war that my country had been drawn into was over, but it continued its relentless destruction. The religion that had been imposed on me offered no explanation. I was told that God acted in mysterious ways and that my father was now with Him. But why did God make my father die? He didn't deserve it, he had been a good Christian all his life, so was his family. My search for an answer took me to the Buddhist temple.

I spent three years studying the sacred scriptures. The words of the enlightened one taught me about karma and it answered my questions. Everything that happened to men was a result of their past actions or present deeds. I didn't know what my father had done in a previous life but I had seen the consequence, and I wanted to break free from the samsara, the continual repetitive cycle of birth, death and reincarnation. The only way to do that was to follow the Buddhist path.

I burnt all the Christian books that were in the house. The only book that escaped the fire was the diary that Émile Vattier had written while he was in Laos. There was something about it that compelled me to read it. At first I didn't believe what he had written about the Vidhi-Vikalpaka, I thought it was a tale he had made up. And then, I made a discovery that convinced me that it wasn't; I found a box with Émile Vattier's initials. There were some crystals inside; Émile had written about their power and how he had used them to build the Vidhi-Vikalpaka, but they didn't look any different to the crystals I had seen before—pretty stones that didn't have the healing properties that some like to attribute to them. However, these crystals were different; as I took them in my hand, I felt them warming up and they glowed. The light was so bright that I closed my eyes and I saw the history and the future of the Vidhi-Vikalpaka."

The Master looked at Guillaume and Sylvie; they were paying attention to his every word.

"I won't repeat what you already know. Your information stops when Émile went to Laos. He bequeathed the Vidhi-Vikalpaka to my grandfather who kept it in a safe place. When the Japanese invaded Laos, they plundered my family's village, and one of the soldiers took it with him. He became a businessman, selling food and drink to restaurants. The Vidhi-Vikalpaka was a just a pretty object to him, and when your grandfather introduced him to the wines of your country, he gave it to him. I saw that your grandfather used it and then locked it away. But when he was going to pass away, it was going to fall into your hands and an evil man was going to try to steal it to make an enormous change, one that was going to destroy the fabric of the universe."

Guillaume said, "That's what you told me in the cave, but I still don't understand."

"There is an equilibrium between forces of creation and forces of destruction, or if you prefer good and evil. The law of karma maintains that balance, but if men escape from the consequences of their actions by changing the past, that law is broken and it creates cracks in the fabric of the universe. I couldn't do anything about the small cracks that had already been made, but I could save the universe from destruction, which would happen if the Vidhi-Vikalpaka fell in the wrong hands. I realised that the result of my past actions was that I had been given this mission and that if I succeeded, I would take my rightful place as the new Buddha. When I went to the monastery and explained this to the monks, they didn't believe me. They said that I was doomed if I continued to take my hallucinations for reality. Then I went to the villages and described my visions. I recruited some disciples amongst those who believed me. But we needed to isolate ourselves from those who in their ignorance could hinder us, and we built this monastery here. I used the crystals to project images around the monastery to scare our neighbours away.

We had the peace and quiet that we needed to accomplish our mission. I found that the crystals also gave me the ability to see what a person was seeing and feel what a person was feeling by concentrating on his name, no matter where he was. This was going to be useful to carry out my plan to make the Vidhi-Vikalpaka return here and destroy it. This is where—"

"Do you realise the suffering you've inflicted on my family to complete your mission? We thought Bénédicte was dead, my parents were close to divorcing—"

"A small price to pay to save the universe, wouldn't you agree? The emotions you felt were a consequence of your attachments, your suffering was completely avoidable."

"Don't you have any emotions? Are you devoid of love and compassion?" Sylvie asked.

"What Westerners call love is nothing more than a chemical reaction. It's an illusion created by your body which itself is an illusion. Do not believe it. Real love cannot be seen, heard or felt. It is not born out of attachment, lust or possession and therefore does not create more suffering. True love does not depend on another being to fulfil or express itself. It is the love of the universe in its entirety, not just our limited circle of parents, children, spouse, family or friends. "

The Master paused and looked at Guillaume and Sylvie. "Now, hand me over the Vidhi-Vikalpaka. It must be destroyed at sunset today. The evil man is approaching, he is ready to take away lives to obtain it, but he waits for the cover of darkness. He will be taken care of and you will be free to leave tomorrow at sunset."

"How do I know you're not bluffing? You made us believe that Bénédicte is still alive, but we haven't seen her. Once I give you the typewriter, you can do whatever you like with it. Which is probably not much, it's locked you know."

The Master glared at Guillaume. "Of course I know that, but what you don't know is that the evil man has obtained the instructions to unlock the Vidhi-Vikalpaka. He is dangerous because he doesn't know what will happen if he succeeds."

He turned his head and raised his voice. "You can bring her in now."

Guillaume and Sylvie got up. A door on the side opened, and a monk walked in, followed by a woman with chestnut coloured eyes and hair that Guillaume recognised instantly. He hoped that weight was the only thing that she had lost during the twenty-two years that she had spent here. Brother and sister looked at each other for a fleeting moment before hugging each other and letting tears of joy flow on each other's shoulder.

The Master interrupted their effusions.

"Do you see now that I was speaking words of truth?"

"Yes, you can have the typewriter now. My sister and I have twenty-two years of our lives to catch up on. Bénédicte, this is my friend Sylvie."

Sylvie hugged Bénédicte. "I've heard so much about you."

Bénédicte guided Guillaume and Sylvie to her room, where Pathana was waiting.

"They forced me to lie to you Guillaume, I wish I had found a way to warn you," Bénédicte said after Guillaume had summarised what happened since the day of her supposed death. "Pathana's brother was the traitor. Pathana had no idea that he belonged to a sect, he thought he was an ordinary Buddhist monk. We were taken here as soon as we landed in Laos. Once a week they took me to Tung Luang Chalerm Phrakiat so I could call you and give you some news. They listened to what I said and they threatened to harm Pathana if I deviated from the script. I had no choice but to lie to you, and I had no way of contacting you. There was no way we could even consider escaping, the Master always knew what we were thinking. We had nothing to do but live the life of the monks, studying the scriptures, praying, working. Pathana and I discussed the master's teachings; we took the good and ignored the crazy, that's what kept us sane. The hardest thing was not knowing how long we were going to be locked up here. I know I shouldn't say this but I was praying that Louis was going to pass away quickly."

"So you knew the Master's plan."

"Yes, and when the Master told me that an evil man was prepared to do anything to get it, I feared for your life. You've done well. Especially you, Sylvie."

"But there's one thing I don't understand. Why did the Master wait so long to get the typewriter? He could have asked us to exchange it for your freedom when he kidnapped you. We would have come here straight away."

"Yes, but where would the glory have been from that? There wouldn't have been an evil man to defeat."

"Speaking of him, the Master said that he is approaching, but I don't see how he could have found us here. If it wasn't for the typewriter and the crystal, we would never have found this place."

"Maybe he's got a crystal too."

"Even so, there's one thing he has that we don't, and that's a gun," Sylvie said.

The noise of the gongs and the diminishing light announced that the time that the community had waited for had come. Sylvie, Guillaume, Bénédicte and Pathana were ordered to attend the ceremony, everyone here needed to be a witness to the salvation of the cosmic order.

A fire was lit in front of the temple. The monks and their guests stood in a circle around the fire, chanting Sanskrit words that Bénédicte translated to mean "Glory to the Master, saviour of the universe."

The Master held the typewriter in his hands, he raised them and said, "Tonight, the Vidhi-Vikalpaka will be no more, men will no longer be tempted to escape from the law of Karma. Those that did will understand that it is supreme.

The consequences they avoided will be restored and the cracks in the fabric of the universe will be mended."

Guillaume realised what this meant. He ran towards the Master and yelled "No, you can't do that, Lien will be killed by the Kampucheans!" He grabbed the typewriter from the Master and the chanting stopped.

"Give it back!" the Master said. Three monks sprang into action to help the Master, but the sound of a gunshot stopped them in their tracks.

"Hand over that typewriter!" Aaron said, lowering his gun.

"No!" replied Guillaume, clutching the typewriter against his chest.

Bénédicte picked up the jar that was going to be used to store the ashes and threw it at Aaron. He ducked to avoid it and fired a shot. She fell to the ground and one of the monks kicked Aaron in the chest. As he fell, Sylvie rushed to grab his gun. Guillaume put down the typewriter and joined Pathana who was kneeling down next to Bénédicte, crying. Guillaume felt her pulse. "She's still alive. Quick get some water and bandages."

"You're a doctor, save her!" Pathana said.

"We have to get her to a hospital. It's too dangerous to remove the bullet here, it may have hit nerves or blood vessels. Where's the nearest hospital?" Guillaume asked.

"At Muang Chiang Rai, In Thailand," one of the monks replied.

"It's too dangerous to move her, we have to call the hospital, they'll probably have a helicopter."

"A helicopter, do you know what that means? The existence of this sanctuary will be revealed," the Master said.

"We're talking about saving a human life here! Which was put in danger trying to stop the typewriter from falling in the wrong hands."

The Master hesitated and Sylvie said, "Your sanctuary has served its purpose, hasn't it?"

"You're right, but someone will have to go to Tung Luang Chalerm Phrakiat. It's the nearest place that has a phone."

"I'll go," Pathana said.

"Anula, go with him," the Master said.

Guillaume carried Bénédicte to her room with the help of another monk, followed by Sylvie who had picked up the typewriter. They laid her on her mat and covered her with a blanket.

Sylvie sat on the floor next to Guillaume. "How critical is she?"

"She was lucky, a few centimetres lower and it would have hit her heart."

"You didn't look like you were going to let go, you could have been shot yourself."

"I was trying to save Lien, and Bénédicte almost lost her life trying to save me."

A few minutes passed while the two friends were deep in thought.

"Guillaume, I know this probably isn't the best time to tell you this, but I don't think there will ever be a right time. I've tried a few times already, but I can't keep this to myself anymore."

"What is it?"

"I'm..." Sylvie took a deep breath. "I'm your half-sister."

Guillaume looked at her in disbelief.

"After your family was told Bénédicte had died, your father had an affair with my mother. He was looking for comfort that your mother couldn't give him, and my mother was feeling neglected. Her husband was on the campaign trail, nothing else mattered to him."

"But how did you find out?"

"When I moved into your flat. My mother thought you were handsome, and she was afraid I would fall in love with you. I told her that you were too old for me, I hope you don't mind. Later I thought that if I had come out before, I would never have known. Without knowing it, you've been an awesome brother to me Guillaume."

"But why didn't you tell me? I thought you trusted me entirely. When you came out to me, you said I was the first one to know."

Sylvie lowered her head. "I did trust you, but I didn't want to mess up your family with my revelation."

"I wasn't thinking only about myself when I said that, it must have been hard to keep that to yourself."

"Actually, it wasn't the hardest thing."

Guillaume widened his eyes. "You mean there's more?"

"My so-called father never loved me. He must have suspected something, although he never said anything, it would have been detrimental to his reputation. Instead, he started abusing me when I was ten."

Guillaume couldn't believe what he was hearing. He put his arms around her shoulders. Sylvie continued in between sobs. "It went on for five years. He said that if I told anyone, it would me my word against his. When I learnt that I wasn't his natural daughter, I thought that it was a justified punishment. It was like he had a right to do it because I had a debt to pay. I was ashamed of who I was, the result of an affair."

"But you can't let him get away with that!"

"What can I do? He has friends in high places, he boasted recently that he had secured an appointment with François Hollande about a possible position."

"When we get back home, I'll speak to Hervé, he owes me a favour."

"Thanks Guillaume, you don't know what a relief this is for me. I'm sorry it was at such a bad moment. It must be a shock for you to learn that you have a half-sister just when you're re-united with your lost sister who's almost killed before your eyes. But you need to focus on Bénédicte now, I don't want to be a burden to you."

Bénédicte groaned; Guillaume got up and poured a glass of water for her. "Don't worry sisters, I can look after both of you."

Three days later, Bénédicte came out of the hospital. Following the doctor's advice to get some rest, she stayed at Tung Luang Chalerm Phrakiat where Pathana joined her. Guillaume, who had gone with her, came back to the sanctuary where Sylvie was waiting for him.

"We questioned the man," Sylvie said. "His name is Aaron Rosenberg and he's a Mossad agent, but he says he isn't on an official mission. He found us thanks to a tracking device he had placed in our backpacks. When I asked him how he knew about the typewriter, he claimed that his mother had an affair with your grandfather who told her about it."

"That makes him my half-cousin. I bet his mother's name starts with M."

"Why's that?"

"I found a painting in Louis's house with the initials M.R. I'm not surprised, we all knew he cheated on my grandmother. It doesn't matter now, the past is the past, you can't change it," Guillaume said with a smile. "Did he say what he was intending to do with the typewriter?"

"He was going to stop the Shoah from happening."

"So that's the enormous change the Master spoke about. I guess that would've stretched the fabric of the universe, but I don't agree with his reasoning that the people who perished had done evil deeds in a previous life. It's absolute nonsense."

"I dare you to tell him that."

"I don't need to, he's probably listening to us now."

"That's creepy, I hope he's going to stop when he gets what he wants."

"That's not going to happen though."

"Oh, I forgot to mention—while you were away, the Master made a proposition: if you give him the typewriter, he'll bury it in a location that no one will know about, and burn Émile's diary. The universe is still saved and so is Lien. He's waiting for your answer."

"It's yes of course. I don't want to touch it again. When I think that if I had succeeded in stopping Bénédicte from going to Laos you wouldn't have existed, I understand why you were trying to stop me."

Sylvie looked at her feet. "Sorry I lied to you about Sophie, it was the only way I could find to stop you from asking Lien to change your past."

"I'm relieved she's still alive. But what's the Master going to do with Aaron?"

"He'll stay here until he's cured of his delusion, his hatred and his greed."

"He's here for a long time then; what about his gun?"

"It's well guarded; it will be buried with the typewriter."

"Let's go and see the Master. I have a favour to ask him."

Guillaume and Sylvie went to the Master's room to give him the typewriter; they waited for him to finish his meditation.

"Master, I have lived twenty-two years of my life believing lies. My perception of the world has shifted. I know that things are not always what they seem to be. Life has its mysteries that will never be solved."

"Buddha taught that suffering is conditioned by a misunderstanding of the nature of self and reality," the Master added.

"But before I go, there's one mystery I would like you to shed some light on. It's about a woman named Lien."

"Yes, I know about her. She was saved once by your grandfather and you saved her a second time. Her life is a crack in the fabric of the universe but it's very small, it isn't a threat. However that crack must be contained. For that reason, she will not be able to bear life in her womb. What do you want to know?"

"She doesn't know what happened to her mother after she was captured by pirates when her family was fleeing persecution, and it's distressing her. I haven't had any visions about her mother's fate, even with the crystal you gave me."

"That's because you're in love and your emotion is interfering with your clairvoyance. What is her name?"

"Kim Nguyen."

The Master closed his eyes and whispered her name. "She didn't suffer at the hands of the pirates. Their boat sailed into the path of a typhoon and sank. They all drowned, including her."

"Thank you Master, I will let her know, she will be relieved that she didn't suffer for long."

"Master, where do you think the crystals came from?" Sylvie asked.

"As you know, Émile found them near his village."

"But before that?"

"What do you mean?"

"Could they have come from another planet?"

"I hadn't thought of that, they have allowed me to see much, but they have remained silent on their origin. And how would they have got here?"

"They could have been brought by an alien being who visited earth and then returned to his galaxy."

The Master struggled to keep a straight face. "Do you think that Émile was right about Jesus?"

Sylvie's ears turned red; she looked to Guillaume for support, but he looked confused. "Well... No... I mean, maybe he saw a man with special powers who looked like Jesus visiting earth."

"I see what you mean. It would explain why these are the only crystals on earth with such special properties." He was pensive. "No sacred scripture that I know evokes the possibility of life in another galaxy. I had never contemplated it, but it doesn't really change anything for me."

"But what if there were planets populated by enlightened beings who didn't know war or violence."

This time, the Master smiled. "If they visited earth and saw how primitive we are, they would go home and never come back."

Guillaume had witnessed a kind of miracle, the first time in his life that the Master had smiled. He said, "Master, one last question, where did my clairvoyance come from? I started seeing the invisible before you gave me the crystal."

"I imparted this ability on you when your grandfather died, by transferring enough of the crystal's energy onto you. I knew you couldn't fulfil your destiny without help."

"And the crystal?"

"I teleported it to convince you that you hadn't dreamt."

"Now that my mission has been accomplished, can I keep the crystal and the clairvoyance?"

"Yes, one does not take away what one has given. How you use them is up to you, but I have faith in you Guillaume, don't disappoint me."

The next day, Guillaume and Sylvie left the temple and went to the hotel where Bénédicte and Pathana were staying. Guillaume called his parents to tell them that he had found Bénédicte; he repeated the news five times to his incredulous mother, before handing over the telephone to Bénédicte who promised that she would be with them in a few days.

"What are you going to do after?" Guillaume asked Bénédicte.

"Pathana and I will stay at least until Christmas and then we'll come back here. We haven't changed our plans. Except for one thing... We'll settle in a place that has decent obstetric facilities. I hope it's not too late, but I want to try and I don't want to risk my life giving birth."

Guillaume smiled and Bénédicte continued, "If it doesn't work out, we'll adopt; there are many children that are in need here. As for you, I don't need a crystal to see where you're going. To a very big island where a woman with a beautiful name and I guess a beautiful face is waiting for her soul mate."

"It's not really what I had in mind."

"You were ready to give your life to save her, I would've thought the first thing you had on your mind was to be with her."

"But we knew our relationship didn't have a future. It's what made our time together so intense. I don't know if we would still love each other with the same passion if we knew we were going to be together for the rest of our lives."

Bénédicte crossed her arms and cocked her head. The look in her eyes unsettled Guillaume who looked for an escape. "Anyway, I'm due back at the hospital now, and I'm waiting for an answer from Doctors Without Borders. There are mothers and babies to be saved you know."

"Yes, but deep inside, is it really what you want to do?"

"Of course, I've been waiting all my life for that!"

"Wait a minute, just step back for a moment and think about why you wanted to do that. Was it really for the mothers and babies, or for you?"

"Of course, it was for them."

"No it was for you. You were hurt by your loss and I understand that. You tried to give it meaning, to put things right in your own way. Saving lives would have made you feel better, but it wouldn't have been enough. Now you know I'm alive, but your wound isn't healed yet, it's going to take time for your mind to adjust to the new reality. But don't wait. Now that you've found the woman of your life, you need to review your priorities. Australia isn't far away from here. Book a flight from Vientiane. If you don't, you'll regret it all your life and you won't be able to dig out the typewriter to fix your life."

Guillaume was about to reply, but a scent interrupted him. He sniffed three times to be sure: *Anaïs Anaïs*, Lien's perfume. He closed his eyes and saw her in her house; she was looking at a photo of them that an obliging tourist had taken at the Nice flower market. She turned her head and smiled. In that brief moment that could not be measured because love is stronger than time, he found eternity.

He opened his eyes and said, "Bénédicte, you're right. It's time I lived in the present. After I thought you had died, a part of me stayed stuck in the moment when I picked up the phone to hear the news from Keona. And then I planned the rest of my life: study, graduate, practice, join Doctors Without Borders, save lives. I thought it would allow me to move on, but far from it—I was trying to make sense of something that I didn't know was a lie. I was doomed to fail; I never even thought about what I was going to do after. I was stuck between the past and the future, never living in the present."

Bénédicte, Pathana and Sylvie listened to Guillaume sharing his moment of enlightenment.

"After I saw the Master disguised as a druid, I grappled with the idea of pre-determined destiny, thinking that there was no such thing. If destiny did exist, I was the one making it up. Now, when I look at all the coincidences that led to Lien and I meeting, I'm not so sure anymore. But it doesn't matter, from now on, I'm going to live one day at a time, and I'm going to grab the opportunities that I can before it's too late."

Sylvie also had something on her mind that she wanted to share. "It feels good to stop living on a lie. I feel freer than I've ever felt. I want to be me, and if anyone's not happy with what I am, it's their problem, not mine. I'm going to have a frank discussion with my family when I get home. Guillaume, you've been a wonderful friend, no matter who you thought I was. You were the first to know I was gay and our friendship grew. Now that you know I'm your half-sister, it doesn't really change anything, because you've loved me like a brother. And that's saying something. I've seen how much you love Bénédicte."

"We're all going to go in different directions now," Guillaume said, "but we all know that wherever we'll be, we'll always be connected. When I think of what the typewriter has done, it deserves its name of transformer of destinies. We've all been transformed in ways that we would never have thought possible, although you probably wish it had never existed, Bénédicte. If it wasn't for the typewriter, you and Pathana would've lived peacefully, you would've had children—"

"Guillaume, the past is what it is, I wouldn't change it even if I could with a typewriter or anything else. Our circumstances are never a problem, what matters is how we see them and what we do with them."

Guillaume looked at his sister, his brother-in-law and his best friend. For the first time in his life he felt grateful for what he had. He was young and healthy, he loved his job, his family and his friends. And more importantly, He was in love and he was ready to let this love take him to the other side of the world to live a new life.

Connect with me

If you've enjoyed reading *Web of destinies*, please leave a review at your retailer and/or book cataloguing website (Goodreads for example). Thank you in advance.

If you want to keep in touch, here's how you can connect with me, I look forward to hearing from you.

- Email: inard@internode.on.net
- Blog: www.dearfrance.net (includes photos of the French cities where *Web of destinies* takes place)
- Twitter: @PascalInard
- Facebook: www.facebook.com/pascal.inard.3
- Linkedin: au.linkedin.com/pub/pascal-inard/a/541/574/

About the author

Pascal Inard was born in Grenoble (France) in 1960. His family migrated to Melbourne (Australia) in 1972 and he came back to Grenoble in 1985. He married Isabelle, had three children and now he is back in Melbourne with all his family.

He has written a book and blog articles on France and a novel in French and now he writes novels in English.

He also manages IT projects for a major Australian bank.

Other books by Pascal Inard

- *Dear France, sweet country of my childhood – Chère France, doux pays de mon enfance*: a tribute to France with beautiful photos, delicious recipes, vintage postcards and posters, stories from the authors' childhood and interesting facts on French places and traditions. A must for anyone wanting to learn more about France or who is learning French, as it is entirely written in both English and French. Available in print on Amazon and other major online retailers.
- *Un dernier roman pour la route* (novel in French): the story of a bestselling author with writer's block who travels the world in a quest for his inspiration. Available in print and eBook on Amazon and other major online retailers

FAQs (Facts, Acknowledgements and Quotations)

The cities and villages described in *Web of destinies* are real, except for Gevrey-Saint-André. It is very much like the wine-producing villages in the Côtes de Nuits region of Burgundy (twenty kilometres from Dijon), which accounts for 24 of the 33 *Grand Cru* wines in Burgundy (*Grand cru* is the highest wine classification in Burgundy; it designates a vineyard known for its favourable reputation in producing wine).

Here's a map of France highlighting the cities where *Web of destinies* takes place.

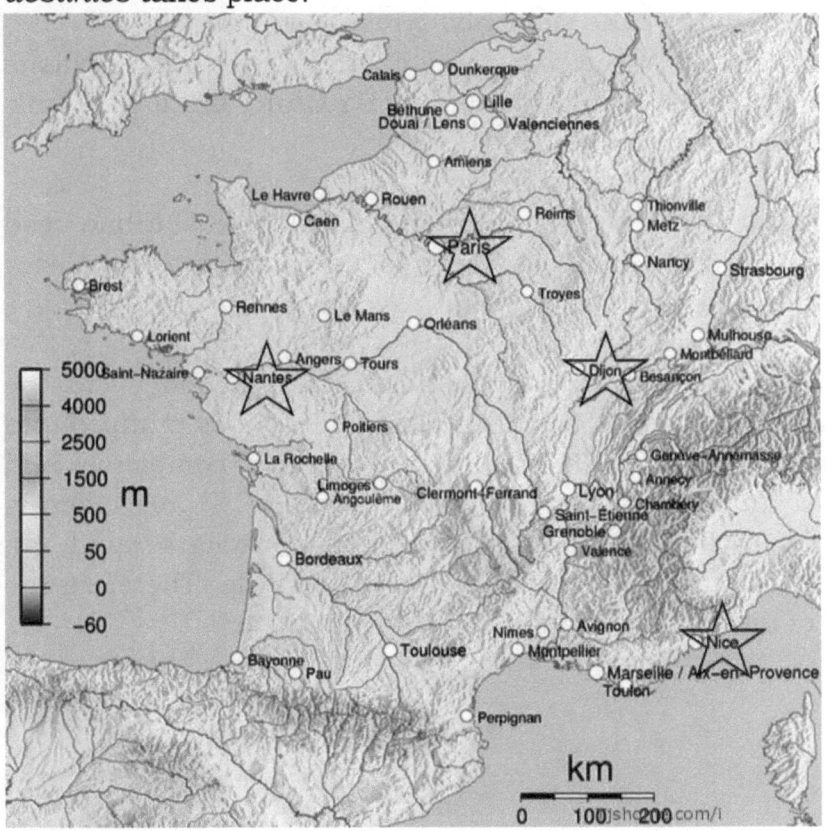

The events described in *Web of destinies* are fictitious, with the following exceptions:

- Chapter 2: the dismantling of a McDonald's franchise that was under construction in Millau in 1999, by the Confédération Paysanne.
- Chapter 3: the performance of Joshua Bell in the Washington subway.
- Chapter 4: the introduction of decimal time (10 hours of 100 minutes of 100 seconds in a day) during the French revolution, which only lasted 500 days.
- Chapter 4: the 2003 summer heat wave that killed 15,000 people.
- Chapter 7: the Goldenberg restaurant attack.
- Chapter 7: the massacre of 3157 Vietnamese civilians by Kampuchean soldiers in Ba Chúc; there were only two survivors.

In chapter 4, Sylvie couldn't remember where she had read that suffering is like gas; here is the full quote by Victor Frankl, Holocaust survivor and psychiatrist, author of *Man's search for meaning.*
"To draw an analogy: a man's suffering is similar to the behaviour of a gas. If a certain quantity of gas is pumped into an empty chamber, it will fill the chamber completely and evenly, no matter how big the chamber. Thus suffering completely fills the human soul and conscious mind, no matter whether the suffering is great or little. Therefore the 'size' of human suffering is absolutely relative."

I am deeply grateful for the following persons and organisations that helped me to write *Web of destinies,* knowingly or unintentionally:

- My wife Isabelle.
- Novelist and writing coach C.S. Lakin.
- My children Amélie, Anaïs and Matthew.
- Best-selling French author Guillaume Musso.
- My parents.
- Metro Trains Melbourne (*Web of Destinies* was written in the carriages of the Frankston line and I was one of the rare commuters who enjoyed the times when my train slowed down or stopped unexpectedly because it gave me more time to write)
- My readers.

Here's what some French writers have to say about destiny:

- A person often meets destiny on the road he took to avoid it – Jean De La Fontaine
- Destiny is what happens to us when we least expect it – Marcel Proust
- Men have invented destiny to attribute the disorders of the universe that they have a duty to govern – Romain Rolland
- Destiny shuffles the cards but it is we who will play them – Bernard Moitessier
- We weave our destiny like the spider its web – François Mauriac
- Our destiny, when we want to isolate it, looks like a plant that you cannot pull with all its roots – François Mauriac

And to finish, a few lines from *C'est ton destin*, a rap song by French comedy trio, Les Inconnus (the unknowns):

Hey Manu! You coming down?

What for?

Er, it's your destiny.

Hey the cops, hey the babes in the RER!

Suburbia is not rosy, suburbia is morose.

So take charge of your own life, it's your destiny!